Coup de pouce pour vous aider à bien comprendre le début de l'histoire...

Nous sommes dans un petit village des Highlands, au bord d'un loch qui regorge de saumons et de truites. Un nouveau groupe entame un stage de pêche à la ligne.

John Cartwright, qui dirige l'école de pêche locale avec sa femme Heather, est un peu nerveux à l'idée de rencontrer les huit stagiaires… et ce jeune policier sans-gêne qui s'invite toujours pour le premier café du stage.

CAST OF CHARACTERS
(in order of appearance)

John Cartwright: Owner
of the Lochdubh School of Casting[1]:
Salmon and Trout Fishing

Heather Cartwright:
His wife, and joint owner[2] of the school

Marvin Roth: American businessman and
budding[3] congressman

Amy Roth: His wife

Lady Jane Winters: Society widow[4]

Jeremy Blythe: Barrister[5] from London

Alice Wilson: Secretary from London

Charlie Baxter:
Twelve-year-old child from Manchester

Major[6] Peter Frame: Ex-army, expert angler[7]

Daphne Gore: Debutante from Oxford

Hamish Macbeth: Village constable[8]

Priscilla Halburton-Smythe:
Local landowner's[9] daughter

Detective Chief Inspector[10] Blair:
Head[11] of Strathbane CID[12]

Detectives[13] Jimmy Anderson and Harry McNab:
Blair's assistants

John Harrington:
Courting[14] Priscilla Halburton-Smythe

Colonel and Mrs Halburton-Smythe:
Priscilla's parents

Mr Johnson: Hotel manager

Angus MacGregor: Poacher[15]

1. pêche à la ligne
2. co-propriétaire
3. en devenir
4. Veuve de la haute société
5. Avocat
6. commandant
7. excellent pêcheur à la mouche
8. Agent de police
9. du propriétaire terrien
10. inspecteur divisionnaire [de la PJ]
11. chef
12. PJ [Criminal Investigation Department]
13. Inspecteurs
14. Soupirant de
15. Braconnier

Day One

Angling[1]*: incessant expectation, and perpetual disappointment.*
– Arthur Young

'I hate the start of the week,' said John Cartwright fretfully[2]. 'Beginning with a new group. It's rather like going on stage[3]. Then I always feel I have to apologize for being *English*. People who travel up here to the wilds of Scotland expect to be instructed by some great hairy Rob Roy[4], making jokes about saxpence[5] and saying it's a braw bricht moonlicht nicht[6] and lang may your lum reek[7] and ghastly[8] things like that.'

'Don't chatter[9],' said his wife, Heather, placidly. 'It always works out all right. We've been running[10] this fishing school for[11] three years and haven't had a dissatisfied customer yet.'

She looked at her husband with affection. John Cartwright was small, thin, wiry[12], and nervous. He had sandy, wispy[13] hair and rather prominent pale blue eyes. Heather had been one of his first pupils at the Lochdubh School of Casting: Salmon and Trout Fishing.

He had been seduced by the sight of her deft[14] back cast[15] and had only got around to discovering[16] the other pleasures of her anatomy after they were married[17].

1. La pêche à la ligne
2. d'un ton plaintif
3. monter sur scène
4. [sorte de Robin des bois écossais, XVIIIe s.]
5. six pence [prononcé par un Écossais supposé près de ses sous]
6. [*fine bright moonlight night*, dit avec des mots de dialecte et une caricature d'accent écossais]
7. [*long may your chimney reek* (id.), puisse ta cheminée fumer longtemps]
8. abominables
9. Ne dis pas de bêtises
10. dirigeons
11. depuis
12. sec
13. clairsemés
14. habile
15. lancer arrière [mais aussi le modelé de son derrière]
16. n'avait pu finalement découvrir
17. qu'après leur mariage

Heather was believed to be the better angler, although she tactfully hid her greater skill[1] behind a pleasant motherly manner. Despite their vastly different temperaments, both Heather and John were dedicated[2], fanatical anglers.

Fishing was their hobby, their work, their obsession. Every week during the summer a new class[3] would arrive at the Lochdubh Hotel. Rarely did they have a complete set of amateurs; experienced fishermen often joined the class, since they could fish[4] excellent waters for reasonable rates[5]. John would take care of the experts while Heather would mother[6] the rank[7] amateurs.

The class never consisted of more than ten. This week they had received two last-minute cancellations[8] and so were expecting only eight. 'Now,' muttered[9] John, picking up a piece of paper, 'I gather[10] they all checked in at the hotel last night. There's an American couple from New York, Mr and Mrs Roth; a Lady Winters, widow of some Labour peer[11]; Jeremy Blythe from London; Alice Wilson, also from London; Charlie Baxter, a twelve-year-old from Manchester – the kid's not living at the hotel, he's staying with an aunt in the village; Major Peter Frame. Oh dear, we had the galloping major before. These men who hang on to[12] their army titles don't seem able to adapt to civilian life. Then there's Daphne Gore from Oxford. I'll send the major off on his own[13] as soon as possible. Perhaps you'd better look after the kid.'

John Cartwright glanced out of the hotel window and scowled[14]. 'Here comes our scrounging[15] village constable. I told the hotel I needed coffee for eight people. But Hamish will just sit there like

1. savoir-faire
2. enragés
3. groupe de stagiaires
4. puisqu'ils pouvaient ainsi pêcher dans
5. des tarifs
6. dorlotait
7. complets
8. annulations
9. grommela
10. crois
11. un pair travailliste [de la Chambre des lords]
12. s'accrochent à
13. le ferai partir de son côté
14. se renfrogna
15. pique-assiette

a dog until I give him some. Better phone down and tell them to set out an extra[1] cup.

'What that policeman needs is a good, juicy murder. Keep him off our hands[2]. All he's got to do all day is mooch around[3] the village getting under everyone's feet[4]. Jimmy, the water bailiff[5], told me the other day he thinks Hamish Macbeth *poaches*[6].'

'I doubt it,' said Heather. 'He's too lazy. He ought to get married. He must be all of thirty-five at least[7]. Most of the girls in the village have broken their hearts over him[8] at one time or another. I can't see the attraction.'

She joined her husband at the window, and he put an arm around her plump[9] shoulders. Hamish, Lochdubh's village constable[10], was strolling along[11] the pier[12] that lay outside the hotel, his hat pushed on the back of his head, and his hands in his pockets. He was very tall and thin and gawky[13]. His uniform hung on his lanky frame[14], showing an expanse of bony wrist[15] where the sleeves did not reach far enough and a length of woolly Argyll[16] sock above large regulation boots[17]. He removed his peaked hat and scratched his fiery red hair. Then he reached inside his tunic and thoughtfully scratched one armpit[18].

The smell of hot coffee wafted up[19] from the hotel lounge below the Cartwrights' bedroom window. It obviously reached the nostrils of the policeman, for[20] Hamish suddenly sniffed the air like a dog and then started to lope eagerly[21] towards the hotel.

The Lochdubh Hotel had been built in the last century by the Duke of Anstey as one of his many country residences. It was battlemented and turreted[22] like a castle. It had formal[23] gardens at the

1. de plus
2. Il nous lâcherait un peu
3. traîner dans
4. à rester dans nos pattes
5. garde-pêche
6. fait du braconnage
7. a bien au moins 35 ans
8. à cause de lui
9. rondouillettes
10. l'agent de police
11. marchait tranquillement sur
12. jetée
13. dégingandé
14. longue carcasse
15. grand poignet osseux
16. à losanges de couleur
17. bottes d'uniforme
18. aisselle
19. flotta
20. car
21. allonger vivement le pas
22. flanqué de remparts et tourelles
23. d'apparat

back and the clear, limpid waters of Lochdubh at the front. It had stags' heads[1] in the lounge, armoury in the hall, peat[2] fires, and one of the best chefs[3] in Scotland. Prices were astronomical, but the tourists came in droves[4], partly because the main road ended abruptly in front of the hotel, making it the only haven[5] in a wilderness of barren moorland[6] and towering[7] mountains.

The village of Lochdubh nestled[8] at the foot of two great peaks called the Two Sisters. It was a huddle[9] of houses built in the eighteenth century to promote the fishing industry in the Highlands. The population had been declining steadily ever since.

There was a general store-cum-post office[10], a bakery, a craft shop[11] and four churches, each with a congregation of about five[12].

The police station was one of the few modern buildings. The old police station had been a sort of damp hut. Constable Hamish Macbeth had arrived to take up his duties a year before the fishing school was established. No one knew quite how he had managed it, but, in no time at all, he had a trim[13] new house built for himself with a modern office adjoining it with one cell. The former policeman had made his rounds[14] on a bicycle. Constable Macbeth had prised[15] a brand-new Morris out of the authorities. He kept chickens and geese and a large, slavering[16] guard dog of indeterminate breed[17] called Towser.

Lochdubh was situated in the far northwest of Scotland. In winter it went into a long hibernation. In summer, the tourists brought it alive. The tourists were mostly English and were treated by the locals with outward[18] Highland courtesy and inner[19] Highland hate.

1. des têtes de cerfs
2. de tourbe
3. chefs cuisiniers
4. en masse
5. seul refuge
6. étendue de landes arides
7. de hautes
8. était niché
9. petit groupe
10. épicerie-bureau de poste
11. boutique d'artisanat
12. cinq personnes
13. proprette
14. ses rondes
15. soutiré
16. baveux
17. race
18. de façade
19. secrète

John Cartwright had been struggling for a month to make the fishing school pay[1] when he had met Heather. It was Heather who had taken over the bookkeeping[2] and put advertisements in the glossy magazines. It was Heather who had trebled[3] John's low fees[4], pointing out shrewdly[5] that people would pay up if they thought they were getting something exclusive and the rates were still reasonable considering the excellent salmon rivers they were allowed to fish. It was Heather who had made the whole thing work. She was plump, grey-haired, and motherly. Her marriage to John Cartwright was her second. John often thought he would never know what went on under his wife's placid brow[6], but he loved her as much as he loved angling, and sometimes, even uneasily[7], thought that the school would not have survived without her, although most of the time he prided himself on his business acumen[8] and his wife comfortably did all she could to foster this belief[9].

He tugged on[10] his old fishing jacket with its many pockets, picked up his notes, and looked nervously at his wife.

'Don't you think we should ... well, meet them together?'

'You run along[11], dear,' said Heather. 'Give me a shout when you're ready to show them the knots[12]. Once you get started talking, you'll forget to be nervous.'

John gave her a swift kiss on the cheek and made his way along to the main staircase. He prayed they would be a jolly crowd. At least he knew the major, although that was more a case of being comfortable with the evil he knew[13].

He pushed open the lounge door and blinked[14] nervously at[15] the eight people who were standing

1. rentable
2. comptabilité
3. triplé
4. tarifs
5. finement
6. front
7. avec même une certaine gêne
8. sens des affaires
9. nourrir cette croyance
10. tirailla
11. Vas-y déjà
12. nœuds
13. mais il n'était pas pour autant à l'aise avec lui
14. cilla
15. en voyant

around eyeing each other warily[1]. A bad sign. Usually by the time he put in his appearance[2], they had all introduced themselves.

Constable Hamish Macbeth was sitting in an armchair at the window, studying the *Daily Telegraph* crossword[3] and whistling[4] through his teeth in an irritating way.

John took a deep breath. Lights, camera, action.[5] He was on[6].

'I think the first thing to do is to get acquainted[7],' he said, smiling nervously at the silent group. 'My name is John Cartwright, and I am your instructor. We find things go easier if we all get on a first-name basis[8]. Now, who would like to start?'

'Start what?' demanded a heavyset[9] woman imperiously.

'Hah, hah. Well, start introducing themselves.'

'I'll be first,' said an American voice. 'My name is Marvin Roth, and this is my wife, Amy.'

'I'm Daphne Gore,' drawled[10] a tall blonde, studying her fingernails.

'Jeremy Blythe.' A handsome, stocky[11] young man with a cheerful face, fair curly hair, and bright blue eyes.

'Charlie Baxter.' The twelve-year-old. Chubby[12], beautiful skin, mop[13] of black curls, remarkably cold and assessing[14] eyes[15] in[16] one so young.

'Well, you know me. Major Peter Frame. Just call me Major. Everyone does.' Small grey moustache in a thin, lined[17] face; weak, petulant[18] mouth; brand-new fishing clothes.

'Alice Wilson.' Pretty, wholesome-looking[19] girl; slight Liverpool accent, wrong clothes.

'I am Lady Jane Winters. You may call me Lady Jane. *Everyone* does.' The heavyset woman. Heavy bust encased in silk blouse[20], heavy thighs

1. avec méfiance
2. le temps qu'il arrive sur place
3. mots croisés
4. sifflant
5. on tourne !
6. C'est parti
7. de faire connaissance
8. on s'appelle par nos prénoms
9. imposante
10. dit d'un ton traînant
11. trapu
12. Joufflu
13. tignasse
14. pénétrant
15. un regard
16. chez
17. ridé
18. colérique
19. l'air en bonne santé
20. un chemisier en soie

bulging in knee breeches[1], fat calves[2] in lovat wool stockings[3]. Heavy fat face with large, heavy-lidded blue eyes. Small, sharp beak of a nose. Disappointed mouth.

'Now we've all got to know each other's names, we'll have some coffee,' said John brightly.

Hamish uncoiled himself[4] from the armchair and slouched forward[5].

Lady Jane eyed his approach with disfavour[6]. 'Does the village constable take fishing lessons as well?' she demanded. Her voice was high and loud with a peculiarly grating edge to it[7].

'No, Mr Macbeth often joins us on the first day for coffee.'

'Why?' Lady Jane was standing with her hands on her hips between Hamish and the coffee table. The policeman craned his neck[8] and looked over her fat shoulder at the coffee pot.

'Well,' said John crossly[9], wishing Hamish would speak for himself. 'We all like a cup of coffee and ...'

'I do not pay taxes to entertain[10] public servants[11],' said Lady Jane. 'Go about your business, Constable.'

The policeman gazed down at her with a look of amiable stupidity in his hazel[12] eyes. He made a move to step around her[13]. Lady Jane blocked his path.

'Do you take your coffee regular[14], Officer[15]?' asked Marvin Roth. He was a tall, pear-shaped man with a domed bald[16] head and thick horn-rimmed[17] glasses. He looked rather like the wealthy upper-eastside Americans[18] portrayed in some *New Yorker* cartoons[19].

1. trop serrées dans des culottes courtes
2. mollets
3. des bas de laine vert amande
4. se redressa doucettement
5. s'avança mollement
6. l'air désapprobateur
7. Elle parlait haut et de façon stridente
8. tendit le cou
9. d'un ton irrité
10. pour nourrir
11. des fonctionnaires
12. noisette
13. la contourner
14. normalement
15. monsieur l'agent
16. chauve
17. de corne
18. riches Américains du quartier chic de Manhattan
19. dessins

Hamish broke into speech[1] for the first time. 'I mostly take tea,' he said in a soft Highland voice. 'But I aye[2] take the coffee when I get the chance.'

'He means, do you take milk and sugar?' interposed John Cartwright, who had become used to translating[3] Americanisms.

'Yes, thank you, sir,' said Hamish. Lady Jane began to puff with outrage[4] as Marvin poured a cup of coffee and handed it over her shoulder to the constable. Alice Wilson let out a nervous giggle[5] and put her hand over her mouth to stifle it[6]. Lady Jane gave her shoulders a massive shrug and sent the cup of coffee flying.

There was an awkward[7] silence. Hamish picked up the cup from the floor and looked at it thoughtfully[8]. He looked slowly and steadily at Lady Jane, who glared back at him triumphantly.

'Oh, *pullease*[9] give the policeman his coffee,' sighed Amy Roth. She was a well-preserved[10] blonde with large, cow-like eyes, a heavy soft bosom, and surprisingly tough and wiry tennis-playing wrists[11].

'No,' said Lady Jane stubbornly[12] while John Cartwright flapped[13] his notes and prayed for deliverance. Why wouldn't Hamish just *go*?

Lady Jane turned her back on Hamish and stared at Marvin as if defying him to pour[14] any more coffee. Alice Wilson watched miserably[15]. Why had she come on this awful holiday? It was costing so much, much more than she could afford[16].

But as she watched, she saw to her amazement the policeman had taken a sizeable chunk[17] of Lady Jane's tightly clad bottom[18] between thumb and forefinger and was giving it a hearty pinch[19].

'You pinched my bum[20]!' screamed Lady Jane.

'Och, no,' said the policeman equably[21], moving

1. prit la parole
2. toujours [écossais]
3. avait l'habitude de traduire
4. manifester son indignation
5. gloussement
6. le réprimer
7. gêné
8. songeur
9. [*please*, en exagérant]
10. bien conservée
11. les poignets étonnamment vigoureux d'une joueuse de tennis
12. d'un ton buté
13. feuilletait
14. comme pour le mettre au défi de verser
15. l'air pitoyable
16. ne pouvait se le permettre
17. bon morceau
18. derrière bien moulé
19. le pinçait de bon cœur
20. m'avez pincé les fesses
21. d'un ton serein

past the outraged lady and pouring himself another cup of coffee. 'It will be them Hielan midges[1]. Teeth on them[2] like the pterodactyls.'

He ambled back[3] to his armchair by the window and sat down, nursing[4] his coffee cup.

'I shall write to that man's superior officer,' muttered Lady Jane. 'Is anyone going to pour[5]?'

'I reckon[6] we'll just help ourselves[7], honey,' said Amy Roth sweetly.

Seeing that there was going to be no pleasant chatter over the cups, John Cartwright decided to begin his lecture[8].

Warming[9] to his subject as he always did, he told them of the waters they would fish, of the habits of the elusive[10] salmon, of the dos and don'ts[11], and then he handed around[12] small plastic packets of thin transparent nylon cord.

He was about to call Heather down to tell her it was time to show the class how to tie a leader[13], when he suddenly felt he could not bear to see his wife humiliated by the terrible Lady Jane. She had been remarkably quiet during his lecture, but he felt sure she was only getting her second wind[14]. He decided to go ahead on his own[15].

'I am now going to tell you how to tie a leader,' he began.

'What on earth's a leader?' snapped Lady Jane.

'A leader,' explained John, 'is the thin, tapering[16] piece of nylon which you attach to your line. A properly tapered leader, properly cast[17], deposits the fly[18] lightly on the surface. The butt section[19] of the leader, which is attached to the line, is only a bit less in diameter than the line. The next section is a little lighter, and so on down to the tippet[20]. Now you must learn to tie these sections of leader together to form the tapering whole. The

1. ces moucherons des Highlands
2. Ils ont de ces dents,
3. retourna d'un pas tranquille
4. en tenant dans ses mains
5. servir
6. Je crois
7. qu'on va se servir nous-mêmes
8. petit discours
9. S'enthousiasmant
10. furtif
11. choses à faire ou à éviter
12. distribua
13. nouer un bas de ligne
14. qu'elle aurait bientôt repris son souffle
15. tout seul
16. effilée
17. lancé
18. mouche
19. culot
20. pointe

knot we use for this is called a blood knot[1]. If you haven't tied this thin nylon before, you'll find it very difficult. So I'll pass around lengths of string for you to practice on.'

'I saw some of these leader things already tapered in a fishing shop,' said Lady Jane crossly[2]. 'So why do we have to waste a perfectly good morning sitting indoors tying knots like a lot of Boy Scouts?'

Heather's calm voice sounded from the doorway, and John heaved a sigh of relief[3].

'I am Heather Cartwright. Good morning, everybody. You were asking about leaders.

'Commercially tied leaders are obtainable in knotless[4] forms,' said Heather, advancing into the room. 'You can buy them in lengths of seven and a half to twelve feet[5]. But you will find the leader often gets broken above the tippet and so you will have to learn to tie it anyway. Now, watch closely[6] and I'll show you how to do it. You can go off and fish the Marag if you want, Major,' added Heather. 'No need for you to sit through all this[7] again.'

'No experts[8] in fly fishing,' said the major heartily[9]. 'Always something to learn. I'll stay for a bit.'

Alice Wilson wrestled[10] with the knot. She would get one side of it right only to discover that the other side had miraculously unravelled itself[11].

The child, Charlie, was neatly[12] tying knots as if he had fallen out of his cradle doing so[13]. 'Can you help me?' she whispered. 'You're awfully good.'

'No, I think that's cheating[14],' said the child severely. 'If you don't do it yourself, you'll never learn.'

Alice blushed[15] miserably. 'I'll show you,' said a pleasant voice on her other side. Alice found

1. nœud baril
2. avec humeur
3. poussa un soupir de soulagement
4. non nouées
5. entre 2 et 6,5 m
6. attentivement
7. d'écouter tout ça
8. Nul n'est expert
9. d'un ton jovial
10. bataillait
11. s'était défait par magie
12. impeccablement
13. n'avait fait que ça toute sa vie
14. de la triche
15. rougit

Jeremy Blythe surveying her[1] sympathetically. He took the string from her and began to demonstrate.

After the class had been struggling for several minutes, Heather said, 'Have your leaders knotted by the time we set out tomorrow. Now if you will all go to your rooms and change, we'll meet back here in half an hour. John will take you up to the Marag and show you how to cast.'

'Well, see you in half an hour,' said Jeremy cheerfully. 'Your name's Alice, isn't it?'

Alice nodded shyly[2]. 'And mine's Daphne,' said a mocking voice at Jeremy's elbow, 'or had you forgotten?'

'How could I?' said Jeremy. 'We travelled up[3] together on the same awful train.'

They walked off arm in arm[4], and Alice felt even more miserable. For a moment she had hoped she would have a friend in Jeremy. But that fearfully sophisticated Daphne had quite obviously staked a claim on[5] his attentions.

Lady Jane surveyed Alice's powder-blue Orlon[6] trouser suit with pale, disapproving eyes. 'I hope you've brought something suitable to wear[7],' she said nastily[8]. 'You'll frighten the fish in that outfit[9].'

Alice walked hurriedly away, not able to think of a suitable retort[10]. Of course, she had thought of plenty by the time she reached the privacy of her bedroom, but then, that was always the way.

She looked at her reflection in the long glass in her hotel bedroom. The trouser suit had looked so bright and smart in London. Now it looked tawdry[11] and cheap[12].

The stupid things one did for love, thought Alice miserably as she pulled out an old pair of corduroy[13] trousers, an army sweater[14] and Wellington boots[15] and prepared to change her clothes.

1. qui l'observait
2. timidement
3. avons fait l'aller
4. bras dessus, bras dessous
5. revendiqué
6. en synthétique bleu pâle
7. de portable
8. méchamment
9. cette tenue
10. réplique
11. voyant
12. bas de gamme
13. de velours côtelé
14. pull
15. bottes en caoutchouc

For[1] Alice was secretary to Mr Thomas Patterson-James. Mr Patterson-James was chief accountant of[2] Baxter and Berry, exporters and importers. He was forty-four, dark, and handsome – and married. And Alice loved him passionately.

He would tease her[3] and ruffle her[4] hair and call her 'a little suburban miss[5]', and Alice would smile adoringly back and wish she could become smart[6] and fashionable[7].

Mr Patterson-James often let fall hints[8] that his marriage was not a happy one. He had sighed over taking his annual vacation in Scotland but explained it was the done thing[9]. Everyone who was anyone[10], Alice gathered[11], went to Scotland in August to kill things. If you weren't slaughtering grouse[12], you were gaffing[13] salmon.

So Alice had read an article about the fishing school in *The Field* and had promptly decided to go. She imagined the startled[14] admiration on her boss's face when she casually described[15] landing[16] a twenty-pounder[17] after a brutal fight.

Alice was nineteen years of age. She had fluffy fine[18] brown hair and wide-spaced brown eyes. Her slim, almost boyish figure[19] was her private despair.

She had once seen Mr Patterson-James arm in arm with a busty[20] blonde and wondered if the blonde were Mrs Patterson-James.

It was not like being[21] in the British Isles at all, thought Alice, looking out at the sun sparkling on the loch. The village was so tiny and the tracts[22] of heather-covered moorland[23] and weird[24] twisted mountains so savage and primitive and vast.

Perhaps she would give it one more day and then go home. Would she get a refund[25]? Alice's

1. Car
2. chef comptable chez
3. la taquinait
4. lui ébouriffait les
5. demoiselle des banlieues
6. intelligente
7. à la mode
8. laissait souvent entendre
9. ce qui se faisait
10. Toute personne d'importance
11. croyait comprendre Alice
12. à massacrer des oies sauvages [d'Écosse]
13. pêchiez
14. stupéfaite
15. décrirait, l'air de rien,
16. prenant
17. poisson de dix kilos
18. duveteux
19. silhouette
20. à forte poitrine
21. On ne se serait pas cru
22. étendues
23. lande couverte de bruyère
24. étranges
25. rembourse-ment

timid soul quailed[1] at the idea of asking for money back. Surely only very common people did that.

Mr Patterson-James was always describing people as common.

Suddenly she heard raised voices[2] from the terrace below. Then loud and clear she heard Mr Marvin Roth say savagely, 'If she doesn't shut that goddamn mouth of hers[3], I'll shut it for her.'

There was the sound of a door slamming and then silence.

Alice sat down on the bed, one leg in her trousers and one out. Her ideas of American men had been pretty much[4] based on the works of P. G. Wodehouse[5]. Men who looked like Marvin were supposed to be sweet and deferential to[6] their wives, although they might belong to the class of Sing-Sing '45[7]. Was everyone on this holiday going to be nasty? And whose mouth was going to be shut? Lady Jane's?

Jeremy Blythe seemed sweet[8]. But the Daphnes of this world were always waiting around the corner to take away the nice men. Did Mrs Patterson-James look like Daphne?

Alice gloomily surveyed her appearance[9] in the glass when she had finished dressing. The corduroys fitted her slim hips snugly[10], and the bulky[11] army sweater hid the deficiency of her bosom[12]. Her Wellington boots were ... well, just Wellington boots.

Carefully setting a brand new[13] fishing hat of brown wool on top of her fluffy brown hair, Alice stuck her tongue out at her reflection and went out of her room and down the stairs, muttering, 'I won't stay if I can't stand it[14].'

To her surprise, everyone was dressed much the same as she was, with the exception of Lady

1. frémissait

2. des éclats de voix

3. sa foutue grande gueule

4. pas mal

5. [romancier humoristique britannique, mort en 1975]

6. pleins de respect envers

7. même s'ils étaient de la promo 45 du pénitencier de New York

8. gentil

9. se contempla d'un air morose

10. moulait ses hanches minces

11. ample

12. son manque de poitrine

13. tout neuf

14. je trouve ça insupportable

Jane, who had simply changed her brogues[1] for Wellingtons and was still wearing the breeches and blouse she had worn at the morning lecture.

'We'll all walk up to the Marag,' said John Cartwright. 'Heather will go ahead in the estate car[2] with the rods[3] and packed lunches[4].'

Loch[5] Marag, or the Marag as it was called by the locals[6], was John's favorite training ground. It was a circular loch surrounded by pretty sylvan woodland. At one end it flowed out and down to the sea loch of Lochdubh in a series of waterfalls[7]. It was amply stocked with trout and a fair number of salmon.

The major took himself cheerfully off[8] to fish in the pool above the waterfall while the rest of the class gathered with their newly acquired rods at the shallow[9] side of the loch to await instruction. Instead of a hook[10], a small piece of cotton wool was placed on the end of each leader.

It was then that the class discovered that Lady Jane was not only rude[11] and aggressive, she was also incredibly clumsy[12].

Although the loch was only a short walk from the hotel, she had insisted on bringing her car and parking it at the edge[13] of the loch. She backed it off the road on[14] to the grass and right over[15] the pile of packed lunches.

She refused to listen to John's careful instructions and whipped her line savagely back and forth[16], finally winding it[17] around Marvin Roth's neck and nearly strangling him[18]. She then strode into the water, failing to see[19] small Charlie Baxter and sending him flying face down[20] in the mud.

Charlie burst into tears and kicked Lady Jane in the shins[21] before Heather could scoop him up[22] and drag him off.

1. mocassins
2. break
3. cannes
4. les pique-niques
5. [lac, en écossais]
6. gens du coin
7. cascades
8. partit joyeusement de son côté
9. peu profond
10. hameçon
11. grossière
12. maladroite
13. au bord
14. partit en marche arrière jusque sur
15. en plein sur
16. donnait des coups de fouet féroces avec sa ligne
17. l'enroulant
18. ce qui faillit l'étrangler
19. sans voir
20. la tête la première
21. tibias
22. ait pu le prendre dans ses bras

'I'll kill her,' muttered John. 'She's ruining the holiday for everyone.'

'Now, now[1],' said Heather. 'I'll deal with her while you look after the others.'

Alice listened carefully as John Cartwright's now slightly shaking voice repeated the instructions.

'With the line in front of you, take a foot or so[2] of the line from the reel[3] with your left hand. Raise the rod, holding the wrist at a slight down slant[4]. Bring the line off the water with a smooth[5] motion but with enough power to send it behind you, stopping the rod at the twelve o'clock position. Your left hand holding the line pulls downwards. When the line has straightened out behind you, bring the rod forward smartly[6]. As the line comes forward, follow through to the ten o'clock position, letting the line fall gently to the water. Oh, *very* good, Alice.'

Alice flushed with pleasure. Heather had said something to Lady Jane, and Lady Jane had stalked off[7]. Without her overbearing[8] presence, the day seemed to take on light and colour. Heather shouted she was returning to the hotel to bring back more packed lunches.

A buzzard[9] sailed above in the light blue sky. Enormous clumps of purple heather studied their reflections in the mirror surface of the loch. The peaty[10] water danced as Alice waded[11] dreamily in the red and gold shallows, which sparkled and glittered like marcasite. She cast, and cast, and cast again until her arms ached[12]. Heather came back with new lunches, and they all gathered around the estate car, with the exception of Lady Jane and the major.

Suddenly, it *was* a holiday. A damp and scrubbed[13] Charlie had been brought back by

1. Allons, allons
2. une trentaine de centimètres
3. moulinet
4. légèrement incliné vers le bas
5. fluide
6. vivement
7. s'était éloignée d'un pas raide
8. oppressante
9. buse
10. tourbeuse
11. pataugeait
12. à en avoir mal aux bras
13. récuré

Heather. He sat with his back against the estate car's wheel contentedly munching[1] a sandwich.

All at once he said in his clear treble[2], 'That is quite a frightful[3] woman, you know.'

No one said, 'Who?'

Although no one added their criticism to Charlie's, they were all bonded together[4] in a common resentment against Lady Jane and an equally common determination that she was not going to spoil things[5].

'Oh, there's Constable Macbeth,' said Alice.

The lanky figure[6] of the policeman had materialized behind the group.

'Those sandwiches look very good,' he said, studying the sky.

'Help yourself,' said Heather, rather crossly. 'Packed lunches are not all that[7] expensive, Mr Macbeth.'

'Is that a fact[8],' said the constable pleasantly. 'I'm right glad to hear it. I would not want to be taking away food that cost a lot.'

To Alice's amusement, he produced a small collapsible[9] plastic cup from the inside of his tunic and held it out to Heather, who muttered something under her breath[10] as she filled it up with tea.

'You obviously don't get much crime in this area, Officer,' said Daphne caustically.

'I wouldnae[11] say that,' said Hamish between bites of ham sandwich. 'People are awfy[12] wicked[13]. The drunkenness[14] on a Saturday night is a fair disgrace[15].'

'Have you made any major arrests?' pursued Daphne, catching Jeremy Blythe's eye and inviting him to share in the baiting of[16] Hamish.

'No, I hivnae bagged[17] any majors. A few sodjers[18] sometimes.'

1. en mordant de bon cœur dans
2. voix claire de soprano
3. effroyable
4. unis
5. tout gâcher
6. silhouette d'échalas
7. si
8. Ah tiens
9. pliable
10. dans sa barbe
11. [wouldn't]
12. très [écossais]
13. vilains
14. ivrognerie
15. vrai scandale
16. se joindre à elle pour asticoter
17. n'ai pas coffré
18. [soldiers]

Amy Roth let out a trill of laughter, and Daphne said crossly to Hamish, 'Are you being deliberately stupid?'

Hamish looked horrified. 'I would no more dream of being deliberately stupid, miss, than you yourself would dream of being deliberately bitchy[1].'

'Fun's over[2],' whispered Jeremy to Alice. 'Back comes Lady Jane.'

She came crashing through the undergrowth[3]. Her broad face was flushed, and she had a scratch down one cheek. But her eyes held a triumphant, satisfied gleam.

John Cartwright hurriedly began to make arrangements to move his school on to further fishing grounds for the afternoon. Boxes of hooks were distributed. More knots demonstrated – a towel knot[4] and a figure of eight[5].

This time even Lady Jane struggled away in silence to master the slippery nylon. The fever of catching fish was upon[6] the little party[7].

'Now,' said Heather, 'we'll issue you each with[8] knotted leaders, but have your own leaders knotted and ready for tomorrow morning. We have the Anstey River for the afternoon. Carry this fishing permit – I'll give you each one – in your pockets in case you are stopped by the water bailiffs[9]. Marvin and Amy, I believe you have done some fly fishing in the States[10]. We'll start you off on the upper beats[11]. We suggest you keep moving. Never fish in one spot for too long. If you come back to the hotel before we set out, then we'll issue you with waders[12]. John and I will show each of you what to do as soon as we're on the river. We'll need to take the cars. John and I will take Alice and Charlie. Daphne can go with Jeremy, and

1. vache
2. Fini, la récré
3. broussailles
4. [nœud de pêche à la ligne]
5. nœud en huit
6. s'était emparée de
7. équipe
8. allons remettre à chacun d'entre vous
9. garde-pêche
10. aux États-Unis
11. tronçons en amont
12. des pantalons de pêche [imperméables]

I believe the rest of you have your own cars. Has anyone seen the major?'

Lady Jane spoke up. 'He was fishing about on the other side of the loch, pretending[1] to be an angler[2]. At least it makes a change from pretending to be an officer and a gentleman.'

'The rest of you go on to the hotel,' said John hurriedly. 'I'll go and look for the major.'

'I wish you were coming with me,' said Jeremy to Alice.

She looked at him in surprise. She had been so obsessed with Mr Patterson-James that she had never really stopped to think any other man might find her attractive.

As Jeremy moved off with Daphne, Alice studied him covertly[3]. He really was a very attractive man. His voice was pleasant and slightly husky[4]. He did not seem to have to strangle and chew his words[5] as Mr Patterson-James did. Her heart gave a little lift[6], and she unconsciously smiled at Jeremy's retreating back.

'No use[7],' said Lady Jane, appearing at Alice's elbow. 'He's one[8] of the Somerset Blythes. Quite above your touch[9], wouldn't you say? Daphne's more his sort[10].'

Alice was consumed by such a wave of bitter hatred[11] that she thought she would suffocate. 'Fook off[12]!' she said, in a broad Liverpool accent.

'Attagirl[13]!' remarked Marvin cheerfully.

Lady Jane muttered something. Alice thought she said, 'I'll make you sorry you said that,' but she must have been imagining things.

Alice was prepared to find herself cut off from Jeremy for the rest of the day. But when they reached the river Anstey, which broadened out at one part into a large loch, Heather arranged that

1. à faire semblant
2. pêcheur à la ligne
3. à la dérobée
4. rauque
5. grommeler
6. palpita
7. Inutile
8. de la famille
9. hors de votre portée
10. genre
11. bouffée de haine mordante
12. [Fuck off]
13. Bravo

Jeremy and Alice should take out the rowing boat[1] and fish from there while the rest were distributed up and down the banks several miles apart[2].

Before she allowed Alice to go out in the boat, Heather gave her a gruelling[3] half-hour lesson in casting. Alice caught her hat, caught the bushes behind, wrapped her leader around the branches of a tree, and then quite suddenly found she had mastered the knack of it[4].

'Don't keep worrying about all that line racing out behind you,' said Heather. 'Just concentrate on what you've been told. Now you're ready to go. Jeremy, you've obviously done this before.'

'Yes, but very clumsily,' said Jeremy.

'Take the boat and row upstream and then drift slowly back down[5],' said Heather. 'You may not catch a salmon but you should get some trout.'

He rowed them swiftly up the stream while Alice nervously held her rod upright[6] and wondered what on earth she would do if she caught a fish. The day was warm and sunny, and she felt laden down with equipment[7]. Her long green waders were clumsy and heavy[8]. She had a fishing knife in one pocket and mosquito repellent[9] in the other, since clouds of Scottish midges were apt[10] to descend towards dusk[11].

She had a fishing net hanging from a string around her neck, and from another string a pair of small sharp scissors.

On top of her wool fishing hat, kept back from her face by the thin brim, was a sort of beekeeper[12] mosquito net which could be pulled down over her face if the flies got too bad[13].

Jeremy rested the oars[14]. 'Pooh, it's hot. Let's take some clothes off.'

1. barque
2. à plusieurs kilomètres d'intervalle
3. épuisante
4. pris le coup de main
5. redescendez lentement à la dérive
6. bien droite
7. encombrée de matériel
8. lourds et la gênaient
9. de l'anti-moustique
10. susceptibles
11. à la nuit tombante
12. d'apiculteur
13. gênantes
14. posa les rames

Alice blushed painfully. Of course he meant they should remove some of their outer woollens[1], but Alice was at an age when everything seemed to sound sexy. She wondered feverishly whether she had a dirty mind[2].

Thank goodness she had had the foresight[3] to put a thin cotton blouse under her army sweater. Alice took off her hat and then her sweater after unslinging[4] the fishing net and laying it in the bottom of the boat. She kept her scissors around her neck. Heather had been most insistent that they keep a pair of scissors handy[5] for cutting lines and snipping free[6] hooks.

'Well,' said Jeremy, 'here goes[7]!'

The water was very still and golden in the sun. A hot smell of pine drifted on the air mixed with the smell of wild thyme[8]. Alice felt herself gripped by a desire to catch something – *anything*.

She cast and cast again until her arms ached[9]. And then ...

'I've got something,' she whispered. 'It's a salmon. It feels[10] enormous.'

Jeremy quickly reeled in[11] his line and picked up his net. 'Don't reel in too fast,' he said. He picked up the oars and moved the boat gently. Alice's rod began to bend.

'Reel in a bit more,' he said.

'Oh, Jeremy,' said Alice, pink with excitement, 'what am I going to do?'

'Take it easy ... easy.'

Alice could not wait. She reeled in frantically[12]. Suddenly the line came clear[13], and she jerked it out of the water[14].

On the end of her hook dangled[15] a long piece of green weed[16].

1. chandails
2. l'esprit mal tourné
3. prévoyance
4. avoir détaché
5. à portée de main
6. couper net
7. c'est parti
8. serpolet
9. à en avoir mal aux bras
10. paraît
11. ramena
12. frénétiquement
13. se dégagea
14. la sortit de l'eau d'un coup sec
15. pendait
16. herbes

'And I thought I had a twenty-pound salmon,' mourned[1] Alice. 'Do you know, Jeremy, I'm still shaking with excitement. Do you think I'm very primitive, really? I mean, I wouldn't normally hurt a fly, and there I was, ready to kill anything that came up on the end of that hook.'

'I don't think you're all that[2] quiet and timid,' said Jeremy, casting again. 'Only look at the way you put down[3] Lady Jane. I heard all about that[4].'

'I can't believe I did that,' said Alice thoughtfully. 'I've never used that sort of language to anyone in my life. But it was all so beautiful when we were having lunch, I wanted it to go on forever. Then suddenly she was there, bitching and making trouble. She drops hints[5], you know. Almost as if she had checked up[6] on us all before she came. She ... she told me you belonged to the Somerset Blythes.' Alice bit her lip. She had been on the point of telling him the rest.

'She did, did she? Probably one of those women with little else to do with their time. I hope she doesn't make life too hard for the village constable. She probably will complain to his superiors.'

'Poor Hamish.'

'I think Hamish is well able to take care of himself[7]. And what policeman, do you think, would rush in to take his place? Hardly the spot for an ambitious man.'

'What do you do for a living[8]?' asked Alice.

'I'm a barrister[9].'

Alice felt a pang of disappointment. She had been secretly hoping he did something as undistinguished as she did.

'What do you do?' she heard Jeremy asking. He was wearing a short-sleeved check[10] shirt and a baggy pair of old flannels, but there was a

1. se désola
2. que vous soyez si
3. dont vous avez rembarré
4. On m'a tout raconté
5. fait des allusions
6. s'était renseignée
7. se défendre
8. comme métier
9. avocat
10. à carreaux

polished air about him, an air of social ease and money. All at once Alice wanted to pretend she was someone different, someone more important.

'I'm chief accountant at Baxter and Berry in the City.' She gave a self-conscious[1] laugh. 'An odd job for a woman.'

'Certainly for someone as young as yourself,' said Jeremy. 'I didn't think such a fuddy-duddy[2] firm would be so go-ahead[3].'

'You know Baxter and Berry?' queried Alice nervously.

'I know old man Baxter,' said Jeremy easily. 'He's a friend of my father. I must tease him[4] about his pretty chief accountant.'

Alice turned her face away. That's where telling lies got you[5]. Futureless. Now she wouldn't dare even see Jeremy again after this holiday.

'When I was your age, which was probably all of ten years ago[6],' said Jeremy gently, 'I told a perfectly smashing-looking[7] girl that I was a jet pilot ...'

'Oh, Jeremy,' said Alice miserably, 'I'm only the chief accountant's secretary.'

'Thank you for the compliment.' He grinned[8]. 'It's a long time since anyone's tried to impress me.'

'You're not angry I lied to you?'

'No. Hey, I think you've caught something.' 'Probably weed.' Alice felt young and free and lighthearted[9]. Mr Patterson-James's saturnine[10] face swam around in her mind, faded and disappeared like Scotch mist.

She reeled in her line, amused at the tugs[11], thinking how like a fish floating weed felt[12].

There was a flash and sparkle in the peaty[13] brown and gold water.

1. gêné
2. de vieux croûtons
3. avant-gardiste
4. Il faudra que je le charrie
5. Voilà ce qu'on gagnait à mentir
6. il y a bien dix ans
7. canon
8. fit un grand sourire
9. insouciante
10. mélancolique
11. par les tiraillements
12. que des herbes qu'on tirait dans l'eau ressemblaient drôlement à un poisson
13. tourbeuse

'A trout!' said Jeremy. He held out his net and brought the fish in.

'Too small,' he said, shaking his head. 'We've got to throw it back.'

'Don't hurt it!' cried Alice as he worked the fly free from the fish's mouth.

'No, it's gone back to Mum,' he said, throwing it in the water. 'What fly were you using?'

'A Kenny's Killer.'

He took out his box of fishing flies. 'Maybe I'll try one of those.'

A companionable[1] silence settled between them. The light began to fade behind the jumbled, twisted crags[2] of the Two Sisters. A little breeze sent ripples lazily fanning out over the[3] loch.

And then out of the heather came the midges, those small Scottish mosquitoes. Alice's face was black with them. She screamed and clawed for[4] her mosquito net while Jeremy rowed quickly for the shore.

'Quick – let's just bundle[5] everything in the car and drive away from the beasts,' he said.

Alice scrambled[6] into the bucket seat[7] of something long and low. They shot off down[8] the road, not stopping until they were well clear[9] of the loch. Jeremy handed Alice a towel to wipe her face.

Alice smiled at him gratefully. 'What about Daphne? I'd forgotten all about her.'

'So had I.' Jeremy was shadowed by a stand of trees beside the car. He seemed to be watching her mouth. Alice's heart began to hammer. 'Did ... did you buy this car in Scotland?' she asked. 'I mean, I thought you and Daphne came up by train.'

1. plaisant
2. amas de rochers tourmentés
3. dessinait paresseusement des vaguelettes à la surface du
4. chercha frénétiquement
5. entassons
6. se rua
7. siège baquet
8. filèrent sur
9. loin

'We did. My father had been using the car. He knew I was coming up this way and so he left it in Inverness for me to collect[1].'

'You've known Daphne a long time?'

'No. Heather wrote to me to ask me if I would join up with Daphne. She had written to Heather saying she did not like to travel alone.'

He suddenly switched on the engine. Alice sat very quietly. Perhaps he might have kissed her if she hadn't kept on and on about[2] stupid Daphne. Daphne was probably back at the hotel changing into some couture number[3] for dinner. Damn Daphne.

'I never thought indecision was one of my failings[4],' said Jeremy, breaking the silence at last. 'I don't want to spoil things by going too fast too soon.'

Alice was not quite sure if he meant he had wanted to kiss her and had changed his mind. She dared not ask him in case he should be embarrassed and say he was talking about fishing.

But he suddenly took one hand off the wheel[5] and gave her own a quick squeeze[6].

Alice's heart soared[7]. A huge owl sailed across the winding road. Down below them nestled the village of Lochdubh.

Busy little fishing boats chugged out[8] to sea. The lights of the hotel dining room were reflected in the still[9] waters of the loch. Down into the evening darkness of the valley they sped. Over the old humpbacked[10] bridge which spanned[11] the tumbling waterfalls of the river Anstey. Along the waterfront, past the low white cottages of the village. Out in the loch, a pair of seals[12] rolled and tumbled like two elderly[13] Edwardian[14] gentlemen.

1. que j'aille le prendre
2. ne s'était pas obstinée à parler de
3. tenue haute couture
4. défauts
5. volant
6. serra furtivement celle d'Alice
7. se gonfla de joie
8. sortaient à petite vitesse
9. calmes
10. bossu
11. enjambait
12. phoques
13. vieux
14. de l'époque d'Édouard VII (1901-1910)

Tears filled Alice's eyes, and she furtively dabbed them away[1]. The beauty of the evening was too much. The beauty of money emanating from the leather smells of the long, low, expensive car and the faint tangy[2] scent of Jeremy's aftershave seduced her senses. She wanted it all. She wanted to keep the evening forever. Scenic beauty, male beauty, money beauty.

A picture of Lady Jane rose large in her mind's eye, blotting out[3] the evening.

If she tries to spoil things for me, I'll kill her, thought Alice passionately.

And being very young and capable of violent mood swings[4], she then began to worry about what to wear for dinner.

When she entered the dining room an hour later, the rest of the fishing party, except for Lady Jane, Charlie, and the major, was already seated.

To her disappointment, the only available seat was at the other end of the table from Jeremy.

Jeremy was sitting next to Daphne and laughing at something she was saying.

Daphne was wearing a black chiffon[5] cocktail gown slit to the waist[6] so that it afforded the company[7] tantalizing glimpses[8] of two perfect breasts.

Long antique earrings hung in the shadow of the silky bell of her naturally blonde hair. Her usually hard, high-cheek-boned[9] face was softened by eye shadow and pink lipstick.

Jeremy was wearing a well-cut charcoal grey suit, a striped shirt, and a tie with one of those small hard knots. He wore a heavy, pale gold wrist watch.

Alice wished she had worn something different. All her clothes had looked cheap and squalid[10]. At last she had settled for a pale pink cashmere

1. les essuya
2. piquante
3. occultant
4. sautes d'humeur
5. en mousseline
6. fendue jusqu'à la taille
7. offrait à l'assemblée
8. un aperçu affriolant
9. aux pommettes saillantes
10. sordides

sweater, a tailored[1] shirt, and a row of Woolworth's[2] pearls. She had persuaded herself in the privacy of her bedroom that she looked like a regular member of the county[3]. Now she felt like a London typist[4] trying ineffectually[5] to look like a member of the county. The dining room was very warm.

Amy Roth was wearing a floating sort of chiffony thing in cool blues and greens. It left most of her back bare[6]. At one point, Marvin slid his hand down his wife's back, and Amy wriggled[7] her shoulders and giggled.

Heather was wearing a long gown that looked as if it had been made out of chintz upholstery[8], but she managed to look like a lady nonetheless[9], thought Alice gloomily. John Cartwright was cheerful and relaxed, obviously glad that the rigours of the first day were over[10].

The hotel had contributed several bottles of non-vintage[11] Czechoslovakian champagne, their labels discreetly hidden by white napkins.

The food was delicious – poached salmon with a good hollandaise sauce. Everyone began to relax and become slightly tipsy[12].

Emboldened[13] by the wine, Alice decided to forget about Jeremy and talk to the Roths. Marvin, it transpired, was a New Yorker born and bred[14], but Amy hailed[15] from Augusta, Georgia. Marvin was her third husband, she told Alice, very much in the way a woman would describe an expensive gown that had been a good buy.

Marvin was quiet and polite and very deferential to his wife, the way Alice imagined American men should be. She began to wonder if she had really heard him shouting earlier in the day, but the Roths did seem to be the only[16] Americans in the hotel.

1. cintrée
2. de supermarché
3. véritable aristocrate
4. dactylo
5. en vain
6. nu
7. remua
8. coton fleuri d'ameublement
9. tout de même
10. passées
11. non millésimé
12. pompette
13. Enhardie
14. pur sucre
15. était originaire
16. seuls

The party grew noisier and jollier[1].

And then Major Peter Frame came stumbling in[2]. His eyes were staring, and his hands were trembling. He clutched on to a chair back[3] and looked wildly around the group.

'Where is that bitch[4]?' he grated[5].

'If you mean Lady Jane,' said Heather, 'I really don't know. What on earth is the matter?'

'I'll tell you,' said the major with frightening intensity. 'I went back up to the Marag this evening, just above the falls[6]. And I got one. A fifteen-pounder on the end of my line. It was a long battle, and I was resting my fish and having a smoke when she comes blundering along like an ox[7]. "Can I get past?" she says. "Your line's blocking the path." "I've got a big 'un[8] on the end of that line," I says. "Don't be silly," says she. "I can't wait here all night. It's probably a rock," and before I could guess what she meant to do[9] she whipped out[10] her scissors *and cut my line.* She cut my line, the bloody bitch. The great, fat, stinking *cow*[11].

'I'll murder her. I'll kill that horrible woman. Kill! Kill! Kill!'

The major's voice had risen to a scream. Shocked silence fell on the dining room.

And into the middle of the silence sailed[12] Lady Jane.

She was wearing a pink chiffon evening gown with a great many[13] bows[14] and tucks[15] and flounces[16]; the type of evening gown favoured by the Queen Mother, Barbara Cartland, and Danny La Rue[17].

'Well, we're all very glum[18],' she said, amused eyes glancing around the stricken[19] group. 'Now, what can I do to brighten up the party[20]?'

1. de plus en plus gaie
2. entra d'un pas chancelant
3. s'agrippa au dossier d'une chaise
4. salope
5. grinça-t-il
6. cascade
7. débarque avec ses gros sabots
8. [one]
9. comptait faire
10. a brandi
11. Cette grosse conne
12. entra majestueusement
13. profusion de
14. nœuds
15. ruchés
16. volants
17. [comédien irlandais travesti]
18. bien sinistres
19. sidéré
20. pour alléger l'ambiance

Day Two

Then as the earth's inner, narrow crooked lanes[1]
Do purge salt waters' fretful tears away[2]
– John Donne[3]

Alice fumbled[4] with a sleepy hand to silence the buzzing of her travel alarm and stretched[5] and yawned[6]. Her room was bathed in a grey light. She had forgotten to close the curtains before going to bed. Fat, greasy raindrops trickled down the window.

Somehow the horrible first dinner had miraculously turned out all right. Lady Jane had carried all before her[7]. Before the major had had time to round on[8] her, Lady Jane had apologized with such an overwhelming blast of sincerity and charm, with such subtle underlying appeals[9] to his status as an officer and gentleman, that the major's angry colour had subsided, and, after that, people had begun to enjoy themselves. It was Lady Jane who had suggested that they should all get together in the lounge after dinner and help each other tie their leaders. It was Lady Jane who had kept the party laughing with a flow of faintly malicious[10] anecdotes.

Alice remembered Jeremy's well-manicured hands brushing against her own and the smell of his aftershave as he had bent his head close

1. de même que les sentiers tortueux de l'intérieur des terres
2. chassent les larmes tourmentées des eaux salées
3. [grand poète du XVIIe s. anglais]
4. tâtonna
5. s'étira
6. bâilla
7. avait triomphé
8. de s'en prendre à
9. en appelant si subtilement
10. légèrement malveillantes

to hers[1] to help her tie knots. He had seemed to lose interest in Daphne.

There was to be another lecture that morning before they went out fishing for the day. Alice got out of bed and went to the window and looked out. She could not even see the harbour[2]. A thick mist blanketed[3] everything and the rain thudded steadily down[4]. Perhaps she would be lucky and would be teamed up[5] with Jeremy again. Alice closed her eyes, imagining them both eating their packed lunches in the leather-smelling warmth of Jeremy's car with the steamed-up[6] windows blocking out the rest of the world.

After a hasty shower, she took out her pink plastic rollers[7] and tried to comb her hair into a more sophisticated style, but it fluffed out as usual.

To her dismay[8], they were not all to be seated at the same table for breakfast, and she was ushered[9] to a table where the major was already eating sausages. Jeremy was with Daphne and Lady Jane at the other end of the dining room.

The major glanced at Alice and then rustled open[10] a copy[11] of *The Times* – last Friday's – and began to study the social column.

'Wet, isn't it?' volunteered Alice brightly, but the major only grunted[12] in reply.

Probably doesn't think I'm worth talking to[13], thought Alice gloomily.

She rose and helped herself to[14] cereal and rolls and juice, which were placed on a table in the centre of the room, and then shyly ordered the[15] Fisherman's Breakfast from a massive waitress who was built like a[16] Highland cow.

When the breakfast arrived, she poked at it tentatively with a fork[17]. Bacon, eggs, and

1. près de la sienne
2. port
3. recouvrait
4. tombait dru
5. devrait faire équipe
6. embuées
7. bigoudis
8. consternation
9. menée
10. ouvrit bruyamment
11. exemplaire
12. se contenta de grommeler
13. que je vaille la peine qu'on me parle
14. se servit de
15. commanda un
16. avait une carrure de
17. y piqua une fourchette méfiante

sausage, she recognized, but the rest seemed odd and strange.

'What are these?' she asked the major. He did not reply so she repeated her question in a rather shrill[1] voice.

'Haggis[2] and black pudding[3] and a potato scone[4],' said the major. 'Very good. Scotch[5] stuff, you know. Introduced to the stuff[6] when I was first in the Highlands on military training.'

'Were you in the SAS[7]?' asked Alice.

'No.' The major smiled indulgently. 'They hadn't been formed in my day. We called ourselves something else.'

'Oh, what was that?'

'Mustn't say. Hush-hush stuff[8], you know.'

'Oh.' Alice was impressed.

'Of course I was in the regular army for most of the big show.'

'Which was ...?'

'World War Two. Can still remember leading my men up the Normandy beaches. Yanks[9] had taken the easy bits and left us with the cliffs. "Don't worry, chaps," I said. "We'll take Jerry[10] this time." They believed me, bless their hearts[11]. Would have died for me. 'Straordinary loyalty. Quite touching, 's matter of fact[12].'

Alice wished her mum could see her now. 'Quite one of the old school[13],' Mum would say.

'Tell me more,' urged[14] Alice, eyes glowing.

'Well,' said the major happily. 'There was a time...'

His voice faded away[15] as a bulky[16] shadow fell across the table. Alice looked up. Lady Jane's pale eyes surveyed the major with amusement. 'Telling Miss Wilson all your tales of derring-do[17]? All

1. aiguë
2. [panse de brebis farcie, spécialité écossaise]
3. boudin noir
4. [galette de pomme de terre]
5. écossais
6. J'ai découvert tout ça
7. Special Air Service [commando de l'armée britannique]
8. Confidentiel
9. Les Yankees
10. les Boches
11. les pauvres chéris
12. pour tout dire
13. Tout à fait à l'ancienne
14. le pressa
15. s'éteignit
16. imposante
17. bravoure

those pitched battles[1] around the tea tent on Salisbury Plain[2]?'

Now what could there be in those remarks to make the major sweat[3]? Alice looked from one to the other. Lady Jane nodded her head and gave a little smile before walking away.

The major looked after her, mumbled something, and went off mopping his forehead[4] with his handkerchief.

Charlie Baxter, the Roths, and all the rest were already in the lounge. A cheerful fire was blazing on the hearth[5]. The heavyset[6] waitress lumbered in[7] and threw a pile of old tea leaves, cabbage stalks[8], and old rolls on the fire, which subsided into a depressing, smoking mess[9].

Heather examined all their leaders and tugged at[10] the knots. Several gave way[11]. 'I wish you wouldn't say you can tie these things when you obviously can't,' said Lady Jane to the major.

'You are supposed to tie them yourselves,' pointed out Heather.

'Like a bloody schoolroom[12],' muttered Lady Jane. 'Oh, here's that wretched man[13] again.'

Constable Macbeth lounged in[14], water dripping from his black cape. He removed it and squatted down[15] by the fire, raking aside the sodden lumps of congealed goo[16] and putting on fresh coal[17] and sticks. Then, to Alice's amusement, he lay down on his stomach and began to blow furiously until the flames started leaping up the chimney.

'This hotel has central heating, hasn't it?' Amy Roth shivered[18]. 'Why doesn't someone turn it on?'

'Now I want you all to try to tie your leaders properly[19] this time,' came Heather's voice. Everyone groaned[20] and began to wrestle with[21] the thin, slippery nylon.

1. batailles rangées

2. [plaine du sud-est de l'Angleterre, terrain d'entraînement militaire]

3. transpirer

4. en s'épongeant le front

5. Un bon feu flambait dans l'âtre

6. trapue

7. entra pesamment

8. queues de choux

9. retomba en une triste masse fumante

10. tira sur

11. cédèrent

12. On se croirait à l'école

13. type

14. entra d'un pas nonchalant

15. s'accroupit

16. gros caillots gluants et trempés

17. remettant du charbon

18. frissonna

19. correctement

20. gémit

21. à s'escrimer sur

1. était allé d'un pas tranquille
2. se raidir
3. était tombé en arrêt
4. Vaincue
5. ciré
6. un pantalon de chasse
7. de bonne famille
8. panier d'osier
9. sortit en flèche
10. parvint à extraire
11. regard hautain
12. Aucune chance de ce côté-là
13. n'en fait qu'à sa tête
14. de la main-d'œuvre bien exploitable
15. En faisant suer le burnous
16. Surveillez votre langage
17. grinça
18. de me débrouiller

Constable Macbeth had ambled over[1] to an armchair by the window. Suddenly Alice saw him stiffen[2]. It was almost as if he had pointed[3] like a dog. He got to his feet, his tall, thin frame silhouetted against the greyness of the day.

Overcome[4] by curiosity, Alice rose quietly and walked to the window. Whatever, or whoever, Constable Macbeth was looking at was absorbing his whole attention.

Alice looked out.

A slim, blonde girl was getting out of a Land Rover. She had a yellow oilskin coat[5] and shooting breeches[6] and green Wellington boots. Her beautiful face was a calm, well-bred[7] oval. She was struggling to lift a heavy wicker basket[8] out of the Land Rover.

The policeman turned around so quickly he nearly fell over Alice. He seized his cape and darted[9] from the room and reappeared a moment later below the window. He said something to the girl, who laughed up at him. He leaned across her and wrested[10] the basket from the Land Rover. The girl locked the car, and then they walked away, the constable carrying the basket.

I wonder who she is, thought Alice. Rich-looking with that cold sort of damn-you stare[11]. Not a hope there[12], Lady Jane would no doubt say.

'This goddamn thing has a life of its own[13],' came Marvin Roth's voice.

'What we need,' said Lady Jane, 'is some useful slave labour[14]. Some *sweated* labour[15], wouldn't you say, Mr Roth?'

'Watch that mouth of yours[16], lady,' grated[17] Marvin Roth.

There was a shocked silence. Oh dear, thought Heather, I should never have tried to cope[18] with them alone. That dreadful woman. She keeps saying things which sound innocuous[1] to me but which seem terribly barbed[2] to the person they're directed against. She's got that mottled red[3] about the neck which usually means high blood pressure[4]. I wish she would drop dead[5].

'And now,' said Heather out loud, amazed to hear how shaky her own voice sounded, 'I will pass round[6] some pieces of string and teach you how to tie a figure of eight.'

To Heather's relief, her husband came into the room. 'We're running a bit late[7],' he said. 'Better get them started. We'll issue them with rods again, that is, the ones who want to rent stuff[8] – I think only the major has brought his own – and then we'll get them off to the Upper Alsh and Loch Alsh.'

Alice pulled on her waders in her room and checked she had everything tucked away[9] in the pockets of her green fowling[10] coat – scissors, a needle (for poking out[11] the eyes of flies – artificial ones, she had been glad to find out – and for undoing knots), and a penknife[12]. She placed her fishing hat on her head and made her way back downstairs, hoping the other guests thought she was a seasoned[13] fisherwoman.

In the car park, John was passing out maps, explaining that Loch Alsh was some distance away. Water dripped from his hat on to his nose. Rain thudded down on the car park. 'At least it will keep the flies away,' he said. 'Now, let me see – Jeremy, you'll take Daphne.' Alice had a sinking feeling in her stomach[14] as John went on to say she was to come along with himself and Heather and young Charlie Baxter. Alice felt Lady Jane's

1. des trucs qui semblent anodins
2. venimeux
3. taches rouges
4. est signe d'hypertension
5. qu'elle tombe raide morte
6. distribuer
7. On est en retard sur l'horaire
8. louer du matériel
9. rangé
10. de chasse
11. faire sortir
12. canif
13. aguerrie
14. boule au ventre

eyes on her face and angrily jerked her already sodden hat down[1] on her forehead.

The journey seemed endless. The mountains were blotted out[2] by the mist. The windscreen wipers[3] clicked monotonously back and forth. Alice looked at Charlie. He was hunched[4] in the far corner. Alice did not know what one talked to children about. 'Enjoying yourself?' she asked at last.

The child's hard, assessing gaze was fixed on her face. 'No,' he said at last. 'I hate that ugly fat woman. She's cruel and mean and evil[5]. Why doesn't she die? Lots of people die in the Highlands. They get lost and starve and die of exposure[6]. They fall off cliffs[7]. Why can't something happen to *her*?'

'Now, now[8],' said Alice reprovingly. 'Mustn't talk like that.'

There was a long silence, then, 'You're very silly, you know,' said the child in a conversational tone of voice.

Alice coloured up. 'Don't be impertinent.'

'*You* were being impertinent,' said the maddening[9] Charlie. 'Anyway, you hate her just as much as I do.'

'If you mean Lady Jane, she *is* very trying[10],' said Heather over one plump shoulder. 'But her faults seem worse because we're such a small group. You wouldn't notice her much in a crowd.'

'*I* would,' said Charlie, putting an effective end to that bit of conversation.

Alice began to feel carsick[11]. The big estate car swayed[12] on the slick[13] macadam surface of the road and cruised up and down over[14] the many rises and bumps[15].

1. enfonça d'un coup sec son chapeau déjà trempé
2. cachées
3. essuie-glaces
4. recroquevillé
5. horriblement méchante
6. meurent de faim ou de froid
7. d'une falaise
8. Allons, allons
9. exaspérant
10. énervante
11. nauséeuse
12. tanguait
13. lisse
14. faisait du roulis sur
15. les multiples cassis et bosses

At last the car veered sharply[1] left and lurched[2] even more over a dirt track[3] where clumps of heather scraped[4] the side of the car. When Alice was just about ready to scream that she was about to be sick[5], they lurched to a halt[6].

She climbed out, feeling stiff and cold.

A rain-pocked[7] loch stretched out in front of her and vanished into the mist. All was still and silent except for the constant drumming of the rain. Heather and John began to unload the rods as the others drove up.

'Now, who wants to row the boat?'

'Me!' cried Charlie, showing rare animation. 'Then you can be my ghillie,' said Lady Jane, a ghillie being a Highland servant[8]. 'Too many bushes around here. I'd be better in the middle of the loch.'

'With a stone around your fat neck,' muttered Amy Roth. She caught Alice staring at her and blushed like a schoolgirl. 'She's such a lady,' thought Alice, amused. 'I bet she feels like fainting[9] any time she says "damn".'

Heather hesitated. Charlie was looking horrified at the idea of rowing Lady Jane. On the other hand, Charlie seemed to be the one[10] member of the party that Lady Jane had so far not managed to intimidate. And he could be rescued after an hour.

'Very well,' said Heather. 'The Roths and the major can go with John further up the loch and fish the river. We should get good brown trout or small salmon so you will only need light rods.'

'What about me?' asked Alice.

'You come with me and I'll start you off,' said Heather. 'Jeremy, you go along to the left and Daphne to the right. Keep moving now. We'll only

1. prit un tournant serré
2. cahota
3. chemin de terre
4. frottèrent
5. allait vomir
6. s'arrêtèrent brutalement
7. criblé par la pluie
8. accompagnateur [de pêche], en Écosse
9. manque s'évanouir
10. seul

fish for a little bit and then we'll meet back here in two hours' time.'

Alice kept looking hopefully in Jeremy's direction while they assembled their rods. Daphne had caught[1] her fly in her jacket, and Jeremy was laughing and joking as he wiggled it free[2] for her.

Alice shivered. The rain had found its way[3] inside her collar.

'Come along,' said Heather. 'No, don't carry your rod like that, Alice. You'll either spear[4] someone or get it caught in a bush.'

Jeremy waded off[5] into the loch, and Alice watched him go until he was swallowed up in the mist. Lady Jane's petulant[6] voice sounded over the water, 'Can't you row a little harder[7]?' Poor Charlie.

Alice waded along the shallows after Heather. 'Just here, I think,' said Heather. 'Try casting here.'

Wet and miserable[8], Alice jerked her rod back and caught the bush behind her. 'No, like this,' said Heather patiently, after she had extricated Alice's hook. She took Alice's arm in a firm grasp[9] and cast the fly so neatly that it landed on the water without a ripple. 'Good,' murmured Heather. 'Now again. And again.'

Alice's arm began to ache. She cursed[10] and stumbled[11] and slipped on the slippery boulders[12] in the water beneath her feet. 'I'll try a little bit further on,' said Heather placidly. 'You're doing just grand[13]. Remember to stop the rod at the twelve o'clock position. The loch's quite shallow for a good bit, so if you move slowly out from the shore, you might get a bite[14] and then you don't have the risk of getting your hook caught in the bushes.'

Why don't I just say I'll never learn how to fish and I don't care, thought Alice wretchedly[15]. Jeremy's not interested in me. I don't belong[16] here.

1. coincé
2. en la dégageant
3. s'était insinuée
4. embrocher
5. partit en pataugeant
6. furibonde
7. plus vite
8. très malheureuse
9. d'une poigne ferme
10. jura
11. trébucha
12. rochers glissants
13. vous en tirez vraiment bien
14. faire une prise
15. lamentablement
16. n'ai pas ma place

But somehow she found herself wading slowly out into the loch, casting as she went.

Then the line went taut[1].

Alice's heart leapt into her mouth[2].

It was probably a rock or a bit of weed. She began to reel in[3], feeling with growing excitement the tugs and shivers on the line. A trout leapt in the air at the end of the line and dived. 'Help!' screamed Alice, red with excitement. Would Heather never come? What if she lost it? She could not *bear* to lose it. Seized with a fever almost as old as the hills around her, Alice reeled in her line.

'That's it,' said Heather quietly, appearing suddenly at Alice's side. 'Get your net ready.'

'Net. Yes, net,' said Alice, scrabbling wildly about[4] and dropping[5] her rod in the water. Heather bent down and seized the rod.

'Get the net ready,' said Heather again. Alice wanted to snatch the rod back[6] but was afraid of losing the fish. Forward it came, turning and glistening in the water. Alice scooped[7] the net under it and lifted it up, watching the fish with a mixture of exultation and pity.

'Quite a big one,' said Heather. 'Three pounds, I should think. It'll make a good breakfast.' She led the way to the shore after removing the hook from the trout's mouth.

'Can't you kill it?' asked Alice, looking at the panting[8], struggling fish. 'Oh yes,' said Heather, slowly picking up a rock. All her movements were slow and sure. 'We'll just put it out of its misery[9].'

How abhorrent the idea of killing things seemed in London, thought Alice, and how natural it seemed in this savage landscape. Heather slid the trout into a plastic bag. 'Put that in your

1. se tendit
2. L'émotion prit Alice à la gorge
3. à rembobiner sa ligne
4. tâtonnant de tous côtés
5. laissant tomber
6. lui reprendre vivement la canne
7. glissa
8. hors d'haleine
9. mettre fin à ses souffrances

fishing bag,' she said to Alice. 'It's about time for lunch. I think I hear the others returning.'

Alice was the only one who had caught anything and received lavish praise[1] from everyone but[2] Lady Jane and Charlie Baxter. The child looked exhausted, and Heather was fussing over him[3], helping him into the front seat of the car and pouring him hot tea.

'You're a marvel[4], Alice,' said Jeremy. 'Did you really catch that brute all by yourself[5]?'

'Yes, did you *really*?' asked Lady Jane.

Alice hesitated only for a moment. Heather was a little bit away, hopefully out of earshot[6]. 'Yes,' said Alice loudly. 'Yes, I did.'

'I'd better keep close[7] to you this afternoon,' grinned Jeremy. 'Seems you have all the luck.' Alice's pleasure was a little dimmed[8] by, first, the lie[9] she had told, which she was now sure Heather had overheard, and, second, by the fact that Jeremy and Daphne were to share a cozy lunch in his car while she herself was relegated to the back of the Cartwrights' estate car.

Lunch tasted rather nasty. Great slabs[10] of pâté, cold and heavy, and dry yellow cake and boiled eggs. But the fishing fever had Alice in its grip[10], and she could hardly wait to try her luck again. Somehow, Alice felt, if she managed to catch another fish all on her own then the lie would be forgiven by the gods above. For the first few moments after they climbed from the cars again, it looked as if the day's fishing might have to be cancelled. A wind had risen and was driving great buffets[11] of rain into their faces.

'It said on the forecast[12] this morning it might dry up later,' yelled John above the noise of the

1. abondance de louanges
2. sauf
3. le dorlotait
4. épatante
5. toute seule
6. hors de portée de voix
7. rester près
8. terni
9. mensonge
10. D'épaisses tranches
10. avait saisi Alice
11. envoyait de grandes rafales
12. à la météo

rising wind. 'I say we ought to give it another[1] half-hour.'

Everyone agreed, since no one wanted to return home without a fish. If Alice could catch one, then anyone could, was the general opinion.

'I'm all right now,' Charlie said, after Heather had towelled his curls dry[2]. 'It was that woman. Row here. Row there. And then she said ... she said ... never mind.'

'Slide along behind the wheel[3], Charlie,' said Heather firmly. 'I really think you ought to tell me what Lady Jane said to upset you.'

But Charlie would only shake his drying curls and look stubborn[4].

Heather was determined to have a word with her husband about Lady Jane as soon as possible. But the roar of an engine told her that John was already setting out with the major for the upper beats[5] of the river.

'Would you like me to run you back[6] to the hotel?' she asked the boy.

He shook his head. 'As long as I can fish alone,' he said. 'I'll wait with the rest and see if the weather lifts[7].'

Alice was oblivious[8] to the slashing rain as she waded out into the loch again with Jeremy at her side, deaf[9] to the sounds of altercation from the shore as Heather told Lady Jane firmly that she was to[10] leave Charlie alone and drive to the upper beats to join the major, the Roths, and John.

'Brrrr, it's cold,' said Jeremy. 'Where did you catch your trout?'

'Just here,' said Alice. 'I'll show you.' She cast wildly and heard the fly plop in the water behind her, then clumsily whipped the line forward[11].

1. devrions essayer encore
2. séché ses boucles avec une serviette
3. volant
4. gardait l'air buté
5. plus en amont
6. que je te ramène
7. se lève
8. indifférente
9. sourde
10. devait
11. fit avancer sa ligne d'un coup sec et maladroit

'I'm tired,' she said defiantly[1], 'and my arm aches. That's why I can't do it right.'

'Look, it's like this,' said Jeremy. 'Keep your legs apart –' Alice blushed – 'with the left foot slightly forward[2]. Bring the rod smartly[3] up towards your shoulder using the forearm and hold your upper arms close to your body[4]. When you make the back flick[5], the line should stream out straight[6] behind, and when you feel a tug[7] at the top of the line, you'll know the back cast is completed[8], and then bring it into the forward cast[9].'

Alice's line cracked like a lion tamer's whip[10]. 'Are you sure you caught that fish yourself?' laughed Jeremy.

'Of course I did,' said Alice with the steady, outraged gaze[11] of the liar.

'I'll try further down,' said Jeremy, beginning to wade away. 'I wonder if Daphne's had any luck.'

Damn Daphne, thought Alice savagely. All her elation[12] had fled, leaving her alone in the middle of a howling wilderness[13] of wind and rain.

She simply *had* to get Jeremy back.

Remembering everything she had been taught, she balanced herself on the slippery pebbles[14] under the water and cast carefully and neatly towards Jeremy's retreating back.

'Caught 'im,' thought Alice. Aloud, she called, 'Sorry, Jeremy darling. I'm afraid I've hooked *you*.'

Now, in the romances that Alice read, Jeremy should have said something like, 'You caught me a long time ago,' and then walked slowly towards her and taken her in his powerful arms.

What he did say in fact was, 'Silly bitch[15]. There's the whole loch to fish from. Come here and help me get this hook out.'

1. d'un ton de défi
2. en avant
3. prestement
4. près du corps
5. ramenez la ligne [d'un mouvement du poignet]
6. bien se dérouler
7. qu'on tire
8. que vous avez fini de ramener votre ligne
9. vous vous préparez à relancer
10. le fouet d'un dompteur
11. regard fixe et scandalisé
12. euphorie
13. désert hurlant
14. galets
15. Pauvre idiote

Blushing and stumbling[1], Alice edged miserably[2] towards him. The hook was embedded[3] in the back of his jacket. She twisted and pulled and finally it came free with a ripping sound[4]. Jeremy twisted an anguished[5] face over his shoulder. 'Now look what you've done. Look, just keep well clear of me[6].' He waded off into the driving rain.

Tears of humiliation mixed with the rainwater on Alice's face. She felt hurt and lost and alone. Her face ached with trying to maintain a posh[7] accent. Jeremy would never have behaved like that with someone of his own class.

She decided to turn about, give up[8], and go back and shelter[9] in the car until this horrible day's fishing was all over.

Alice stumbled towards the shore[10]. Suddenly the water turned gold. Sparkling[11] gold with red light dancing in the peaty ripples. She turned and looked towards the west. Blue sky was spreading rapidly over the heavens. Mountains stood up, sharp and prehistoric with their twisted, deformed shapes. Heather[12] blazed[13] in great, glorious clumps[14], and the sun beat down on Alice's sopping[15] hat.

'Alice! Alice!' Jeremy was churning towards her through the water[16], holding up[17] a fairly[18] small trout.

'Marvellous girl.' He beamed[19]. 'Knew you would bring me luck.' He threw his arms around her, slapping her on the back of the head with his dead trout as he did so.

Transported from hell to heaven, Alice smiled back. 'Come along,' said Jeremy. 'I've got a flask of brandy[20] in the car. Let's take a break and celebrate.'

1. cahin-caha
2. avança à petits pas tristes
3. pris
4. bruit de déchirure
5. douloureux
6. gardez vos distances
7. distingué
8. abandonner
9. s'abriter
10. partit à pas chancelants vers la rive
11. étincelant
12. La bruyère
13. flamboyait
14. touffes
15. dégouttant de pluie
16. faisait des remous dans l'eau en venant vers elle à grands pas
17. brandissant
18. plutôt
19. avait un sourire radieux
20. cognac

While Jeremy got his flask, Alice took off her hat and her wet coat and put them both on the bushes to dry. Jeremy sat down on a rock beside her and handed her the flask and she choked over[1] an enormous gulp[2] of brandy.

The liqueur shot down to her stomach and up to her brain. She felt dizzy with[3] happiness. They had had their first quarrel, she thought dreamily. How they would laugh about it after they were married!

Elated with brandy and sunshine, they cheerfully agreed to return to the loch and try their luck again. And Alice did try. Very hard. If only she could catch a fish all by herself then she could be easy in her conscience.

But at four in the afternoon, Heather appeared to call them to the cars. They were to return to the hotel for another fishing lecture. Even Alice felt sulkily[4] that it was all too much like being back at school. Why waste a perfectly good afternoon sitting indoors in a stuffy[5] hotel lounge?

But none of them had quite realized how tired they were until John Cartwright began his lecture on fly tying[6]. Despite the heat from the sun pouring in[7] the long windows, a log fire was burning, its flames bleached pale[8] by the sunlight. A bluebottle[9] buzzed against the windows.

While Heather's nimble[10] fingers demonstrated the art of fly tying, John discoursed on the merits of wet and dry flies. Names like Tup's Indispensable, Little Claret, Wickman's Fancy, Black Pennell and Cardinal floated like dust motes[11] on the hot, somnolent air. 'Sound like racehorses[12],' said Jeremy sleepily[13].

Alice felt her eyes beginning to close. The major was asleep, twitching[14] in his armchair like an old

1. s'étouffa avec
2. gorgée
3. étourdie de
4. se dit avec mauvaise humeur
5. étouffant
6. comment attacher la mouche
7. entrant à flots par
8. décolorées
9. mouche bleue
10. agiles
11. des grains de poussière
12. des noms de chevaux de course
13. d'un ton ensommeillé
14. tressautant

dog; the Roths were leaning together, joined by fatigue into a fireside picture of a happily married couple. Lady Jane had her eyes half closed, like a basking[1] lizard, and Daphne Gore was painting her nails vermillion.

Suddenly Alice jerked her eyes open[2]. There was a feeling of fear in the room, fear mixed with malice[3].

While John droned on[4], Heather had stopped her demonstration to flip through the post[5]. She was sitting very still, holding an airmail[6] letter in her plump hands. She raised her eyes and looked at Lady Jane. Lady Jane raised her heavy lids and smiled. It was not a nice smile. Heather's face had gone putty-coloured[7]. She put a hand on her husband's sleeve and passed him the letter. He glanced at it and then began to read it closely[8], his lips folded into a grim[9] line.

'Class dismissed[10],' he said at last, putting down the letter and assuming a rather ghastly air of levity[11].

'What was all that about?' murmured Jeremy to Alice. 'And why do I feel it has something to do with Lady Jane?'

'Care for[12] a drink before dinner, Jeremy?' came Daphne's cool voice.

'Are you paying?' asked Jeremy, his face crinkling up in a smile.

'What's this? Men's lib[13]?' Daphne slid her arm into his and they left the lounge together. Alice stood stock still[14], biting her lip.

'I told you you were wasting[15] your time.' Lady Jane's large bulk hove up[16] on Alice's port side[17].

Fury like bile nearly choked[18] Alice. 'You are a horrible, unpleasant woman,' she grated.

1. au soleil
2. rouvrit brutalement les yeux
3. teintée de malveillance
4. continuait de pérorer
5. parcourir le courrier
6. par avion
7. viré au gris pâle
8. attentivement
9. dure
10. Terminé
11. se donnant un faux air dégagé assez terrifiant
12. Que diriez-vous d'
13. La libération de l'homme
14. figée
15. perdiez
16. se dressa
17. à sa gauche [à bâbord]
18. faillit faire s'étrangler

This seemed to increase Lady Jane's good humour. 'Now, now,' she purred[1]. 'Little girls in glass houses shouldn't throw stones[2]. And I *do* trust our stone-throwing days are over[3].'

Alice gazed at her in terror. She *knew*. She would tell Jeremy. She would tell *everybody*.

She turned and ran and did not stop running until she reached her room. She threw herself face down on the bed and cried and cried until she could cry no more. And then she became conscious of all that barbaric wilderness of Highland moor and mountain outside. Accidents happened. Anything could happen. Alice pictured[4] Lady Jane's heavy body plummeting down[5] into a salmon pool, her fat face lifeless, turned upwards in the brown, peaty[6] water. Abruptly, she fell asleep.

When she awoke, she thought it was still early because of the daylight outside, forgetting about the long light of a northern Scottish summer.

Then she saw it was ten o'clock. With a gasp[7], she hurtled[8] from the bed and washed and changed. But when she went down to the dining room, it was to find that dinner was over and she had to put up with[9] sandwiches served in the bar. Everyone seemed to have gone to bed. The barman informed her that the fat FEB had gone out walking and perhaps the other was with her – that Lady Whatsername[10]. Alice asked curiously what a FEB was but the bartender said hurriedly he 'shouldnae hae[11] said that' and polished glasses furiously.

Charlie Baxter threw leaves into the river Anstey from the humpbacked[12] bridge and watched them being churned into the boiling water[13] and then tossed up again on their turbulent road to the sea. His aunt, Mrs Pargeter, thought he was

1. ronronna-t-elle
2. Vous êtes mal placée, ma petite, pour me jeter la pierre
3. j'espère bien que nous avons passé l'âge
4. s'imagina
5. tombant lourdement
6. tourbeuse
7. hoquet
8. sauta
9. se contenter de
10. Machin-chose
11. [shoudn't have]
12. en dos d'âne
13. pris dans les remous

safely in bed[1], but he had put on his clothes and climbed out of the window. His mother had written to say she would be arriving at the end of the week. Charlie looked forward to her visit and dreaded it[2] at the same time. He still could not quite believe he would never see his father again. Mother had won custody of him[3] in a violent divorce case and talked endlessly about defying the law and keeping Charlie away from his father for life[4]. Charlie felt miserably that it was somehow[5] all his fault; that if he had been a better child then his parents might have stayed together. He turned from the bridge and headed towards the hotel.

The sky and sea were pale grey, setting off[6] the black twisted shapes of the mountains crouched[7] behind the village.

Charlie walked along the harbour, watching the men getting ready for their night's fishing. He was debating asking one of them if he could go along and was just rejecting the idea as hopeless – for surely they would demand permission from his aunt – when a soft voice said behind him, 'Isn't it time you were in bed, young man?'

Charlie glanced up. The tall figure[8] of Constable Macbeth loomed up[9] in the dusk. 'I was just going home,' muttered Charlie.

'Well, I'll just take a bit of a walk with you. It's a grand night[10].'

'As a matter of fact, my aunt doesn't know I'm out,' said Charlie.

'Then we would not want to be upsetting[11] Mrs Pargeter,' said Hamish equably[12]. 'But we'll take a wee dauner[13] along the front.'

As Hamish Macbeth was turning away, a voice sounded from an open window of the hotel, 'Throw the damn thing away. It's like poison.'

1. bien au chaud dans son lit
2. l'appréhendait
3. obtenu la garde
4. pour toujours
5. d'une façon ou d'une autre
6. soulignant
7. tapies
8. silhouette
9. se dressait
10. La soirée est belle
11. on ne va pas contrarier
12. d'un ton uni
13. petit tour

Mrs Cartwright, thought Charlie. Then came John Cartwright's voice, 'Oh, very well. But you're worrying overmuch[1]. I'll throw this in the loch and then we can maybe get a night's sleep.'

A crumpled[2] piece of blue paper sailed past Charlie's head and landed on the oily stones of the beach. The tide[3] was out[4].

Charlie picked it up. It was a crumpled airmail. 'You shouldn't look at other people's correspondence,' said Hamish Macbeth severely, 'even though they may have chucked it away[5].'

'I wasn't going to read it. It's got a lovely stamp[6]. Austrian[7].'

They passed the Roths, who were walking some distance apart. Marvin's face was flushed[8] and Amy's mouth was turned down at the corners. 'Hi!' said Marvin, forcing a smile.

'It's a grand night,' remarked the policeman. The American couple went on their way, and Charlie hurriedly thrust[9] the airmail into his pocket.

When they reached his aunt's house, Charlie said shyly, 'Do you mind leaving me here? I know how to get in without waking her.'

Hamish Macbeth nodded[10], but waited at the garden gate until the boy disappeared around the side of the house.

Then he made his way home to his own house where his dog, Towser, gave him a slavering[11] welcome. Hamish absentmindedly stroked[12] the animal's rough coat[13]. There was something about this particular fishing class that was making him uneasy.

1. t'inquiètes trop
2. froissé
3. marée
4. basse
5. l'ont jetée
6. timbre
7. autrichien
8. empourpré
9. fourra vivement
10. acquiesça
11. baveux
12. caressa distraitement
13. pelage rêche

Day Three

Thy tongue imagineth wickedness[1]*: and with lies thou cuttest like a sharp razor*[2].

– The Psalms

Alice had reasoned herself into an optimistic frame of mind[3], although anxiety had first roused her at six in the morning. She had dressed and had taken herself out[4] on a walk up the hill behind the hotel.

A light, gauzy mist[5] lay on everything, pearling the long grass and wild thyme[6], lying on the rippling silk[7] of the loch, and drifting around the gnarled[8] trunks of old twisted pines, last remnants of the Caledonian forest. Harebells[9] shivered as Alice moved slowly through the grass, and a squirrel looked at her curiously before darting[10] up a tree.

Alice sat on a rock and talked severely to herself. The youthful peccadillo[11] that had landed her briefly in the juvenile court[12] was something buried in the mists of time. Why,[13] her mother's neighbours in Liverpool hardly remembered it! It was certainly something that Lady Jane could *not* know about. It had appeared in the local paper[14], circulation eight thousand[15], in a little paragraph at the bottom of page two. At the time, it had seemed as if the eyes and the ears of the world's press had been on her when she had read that

1. Ta langue envisage la vilenie

2. par tes mensonges tu coupes comme un rasoir affilé

3. s'était convaincue de positiver

4. était sortie

5. brume diaphane

6. le serpolet

7. soie ondoyante

8. noueux

9. Des campanules

10. de filer

11. incartade de jeunesse

12. tribunal pour enfants

13. Enfin quoi, [même]

14. journal

15. tiré à 8 000 exemplaires

little paragraph. But now she was older and wiser and knew that she had been of no interest whatsoever to[1] the media. That was the hell of being so hypersensitive. You began to think people meant all sorts of things because of their lightest remarks. Who was Lady Jane anyway? Just some silly, bitchy, discontented housewife. Jeremy had said she had been married to Lord John Winters, a choleric backbencher[2] in Wilson's government, who had died of a heart attack only two months after he had received his peerage[3] for nameless[4] services.

Then there was Daphne Gore. Alice envied Daphne's obvious money and cool poise[5]. Lady Jane hadn't been able to get at her[6]. But she, Alice, must not let her own silly snobbery stand in the way[7] of luring[8] Jeremy away from Daphne. Come to think of it[9], Lady Jane had not riled[10] Jeremy either. Perhaps that was what money and a public school[11] gave you – armour plating[12].

John Cartwright awoke with an unaccustomed feeling of dread[13]. Certainly, he was used to enduring a bit of stage fright[14] before the beginning of each new fishing class, but that soon disappeared, leaving him with only the heady[15] pleasure of being paid for communicating to others his hobby and his passion ... fishing.

Now Lady Jane loomed[16] like a fat thundercloud on the horizon.

Perhaps he was taking the whole thing too seriously. But neither he nor Heather had really performed their duties very well this week. Usually, they meticulously took their class through[17] more intensive instruction on casting, leader tying, fly tying and the habits of the wily[18] salmon. But

1. n'avait pas intéressé du tout
2. député de base
3. sa pairie
4. obscurs
5. calme assurance
6. l'atteindre
7. l'empêcher
8. attirer
9. À bien y penser
10. fâché
11. école privée réputée
12. une carapace
13. crainte
14. trac
15. enivrant
16. planait, menaçante
17. dispensaient à leurs stagiaires
18. rusé

so far both of them had been only too glad to get their charges[1] out on the water, as if spreading them as far apart as possible[2] could diffuse[3] the threatening atmosphere. There was nothing they could do – legally – to protect themselves from Lady Jane. There were two alternatives. They could pray – or they could murder Lady Jane. But John did not believe in God, and he shrank from[4] the idea of violence. Lady Jane had been charming at dinner last night and seemed to be enjoying herself. Perhaps he could appeal to her better nature[5] ... if she had one.

The mist was burning off[6] the loch when the class assembled in the lounge. It promised to be a scorching[7] day. Alice was wearing a blue-and-white gingham[8] blouse with a pair of brief white cotton shorts that showed her long, slim legs to advantage. She was wearing a cheap, oversweet perfume that delighted Jeremy's nostrils. Women who wore cheap scent always seemed so much more approachable, conjuring up memories[9] of tumbled flannel sheets[10] in bedsitting rooms[11]. She was concentrating on practising to tie knots, her fine, fluffy brown hair falling over her forehead. He went to sit beside her on the sofa, edging close to her so[12] that his thigh[13] touched her bare legs. Alice flushed, and her hands trembled a little. 'You look delicious this morning,' murmured Jeremy and put a hand lightly on her knee. Alice realized, all in that delightful moment, that her knees could blush.

'I am so glad to meet a young man who actually pursues single girls[14],' commented Lady Jane to the world at large[15]. 'I'm one of those old-fashioned women who believe adultery to be a sin[16], the next worst thing to[17] seducing servants[18].'

1. élèves
2. les écarter le plus possible les uns des autres
3. calmer
4. répugnait à
5. en appeler à son côté bienveillant
6. se dissipait sur
7. torride
8. en vichy
9. rappelant des souvenirs
10. draps de flanelle froissés
11. des meublés
12. se collant si près
13. cuisse
14. fait la cour à des jeunes filles célibataires
15. à la cantonade
16. un péché
17. presque aussi grave que
18. un domestique

This remark, which sounded like something from *Upstairs Downstairs*[1], went largely unnoticed, but it had an odd effect on both Jeremy and Daphne Gore. Jeremy slowly removed his hand from Alice's knee and sat very still. Daphne dropped her coffee cup and swore[2]. 'No good comes of it[3],' pursued Lady Jane. 'I've known girls run off and make fools of themselves[4] with Spanish waiters and young men who seduce married barmaids. Disgusting!'

There was a long silence. Daphne's distress was all too evident, and Jeremy looked sick.

'Of course,' came Constable Macbeth's soft Highland voice, 'some of us are protected from the sins of the flesh[5] by our very age[6] and appearance. Would not you say so, Lady Jane?'

'Are you trying to insult me, Officer?'

'Not I. I would be in the way of thinking that it would be an almost impossible thing to do.' Lady Jane's massive bosom swelled under the thin puce[7] silk of her blouse. She's like the Hulk, thought Alice. Any moment now she's going to turn green and explode.

'Were I not aware[8] of the impoverished circumstances[9] of your family,' said Lady Jane, 'I would stop you from scrounging[10] coffee. Six little brothers and sisters to support[11], eh? And your aged parents in Ross and Cromarty? So improvident[12] to have children when one is middle-aged. They can turn out retarded[13], you know.'

'Better they turn out retarded – although they're not – than grow up into a silly, fat, middle-aged, barren[14] bitch[15] like yourself,' said Hamish with a sweet smile.

1. [série TV anglaise sur les maîtres et domestiques d'une grande maison]
2. poussa un juron
3. Il n'en sort rien de bon
4. se couvrir de ridicule
5. péchés de la chair
6. de par notre âge avancé
7. pourpre
8. Si je n'étais pas au fait
9. pauvreté
10. de quémander
11. à soutenir
12. imprévoyant
13. attardés
14. stérile
15. garce

'You will suffer for this,' howled[1] Lady Jane. 'Don't you know who I am? Don't you know the power I have?'

'No,' said Amy Roth flatly[2]. 'We don't.'

Lady Jane opened and shut her mouth like a landed[3] trout.

'That's right, honey[4],' said Marvin Roth. 'You can huff[5] and you can puff[6], but you ain't gonna blow any houses[7] down here. You can make other folks' lives a misery[8] with your snide[9] remarks, but I'm a New Yorker, born and bred, and Amy here's a Blanchard of the Augusta, Georgia, Blanchards and you won't find a tougher[10] combination than that.'

A strange change came over[11] Lady Jane. One minute she looked about to suffer the same fate[12] as her late husband[13]; the next, her angry colour had died and she looked around lovingly at[14] Amy.

'Dear me,' she said sweetly, 'a Blanchard born and bred?'

'Yes, ma'am,' said Marvin Roth proudly. 'Amy's *old* money, just like the Rockefellers.'

'Please!' called John Cartwright. 'Let me begin or we'll never get the day started.'

They shuffled[15] their chairs into a semicircle. Heather unrolled a screen and then started setting up a small projector. 'Lantern slides[16],' groaned Lady Jane.

A tic appeared in John's left cheek, but he gamely[17] went on with his lecture, showing slides of what salmon looked like when they headed up river from the sea[18], when they were spawning[19], and when they were returning to the sea.

'Our prices at this school are very reasonable,' said John. '*Very* reasonable,' he repeated firmly after Lady Jane snorted[20]. 'The better-class

1. hurla
2. sans ambages
3. hors de l'eau
4. chérie
5. souffler
6. tempêter
7. ne détruirez aucune maison
8. pourrir la vie de certains
9. perfides
10. plus robuste
11. s'opéra chez
12. sort
13. feu son mari
14. se tournait avec amour
15. poussèrent
16. Des diapositives
17. bravement
18. remontaient le fleuve
19. frayaient
20. un ricanement de lady Jane

salmon beats[1] are all strictly preserved[2] and can only usually be fished at enormous cost. Salmon are fly-caught[3], particularly the ones of small size, on ordinary reservoir-strength trout rods[4]. Regular salmon anglers, however, also include in their tackle[5] longer rods, some designed for two-handed casting[6], larger reels, heavier lines, stouter[7] leaders, and flies much bigger on average[8] than those used for trout.'

'If we had a decent[9] government in power,' interrupted Lady Jane, 'instead of that Thatcher woman's dictatorship, then *everyone* would be able to fish for salmon, even the common people.'

John sighed and signalled[10] to Heather to pack up[11] the projector. He and Heather loved the Sutherland countryside, and he usually ended his talk by showing beautiful colour slides of rivers and mountains and lochs. But he felt beauty would be wasted on the present gathering[12]. 'We will fish the Upper Sutherland today. Heather will pass around maps. The pools on the upper river are small, easy to fish, closely grouped together[13] and within easy distance of the road. During the summer, the fish cannot get over the Sutherland falls and so that's why they concentrate in the upper beats[14]. On your map, you will see the Slow Pool marked. This is a very good holding pool[15], but it is particularly good in high water when it is best fished from the right bank[16]. Heather and I will take Alice and Charlie and the rest of you can follow as before.'

The day was gloriously[17] hot, and even Charlie Baxter lost his customary reserve and whistled cheerfully as the large estate car swung around the hairpin bends[18] of the Highland roads. At one point a military plane roared overhead, flying so

1. secteurs
2. protégés
3. se pêchent à la mouche
4. avec de simples cannes qui suffisent pour les truites élevées en bassin
5. attirail
6. le lancer à deux mains
7. plus robustes
8. en moyenne
9. correct
10. fit signe
11. de ranger
12. assemblée
13. proches les unes des autres
14. zones plus en amont
15. bassin de rétention
16. rive droite
17. merveilleusement
18. virages en épingle à cheveux

low the noise of its jets was deafening[1]. 'A Jaguar!' said Charlie.

John fiddled[2] with the knobs[3] of the car radio. A blast of Gaelic keening[4] split the air. He tried again. Gaelic. 'Isn't there anything in English?' asked Alice, feeling the more cut off[5] from civilization by the sound of that incomprehensible tongue coming from the radio. 'She's got a ticket to ride' roared the Beatles, and everyone laughed and joined in. There was something about the scorching sun and clear air that reduced the likes of Lady Jane[6] to a dot on the horizon. Alice could now well understand why people once[7] thought the night hideous with evil creatures.

Alice was only sorry the estate car was big enough to take their rods lying down flat in the back. It would have been jolly[8] to have them poking upright out[9] of the open window, advertising to the world at large[10] that she was a professional fisher of salmon.

They parked in a disused quarry[11] and climbed out to meet the others. Lady Jane was wearing a Greek fisherman's hat that gave her fleshy face with its curved beak of a nose[12] an oddly hermaphroditic appearance.

John spread out the map on the bonnet[13] of the car and sorted them out into pairs[14]. Daphne and Lady Jane were to fish the Calm Pool, a good holding pool, and were told that the streamy[15] water at the top was best. The major and Jeremy were to try their chances at the Slow Pool; the Roths at the Silver Bank; and Alice and Charlie at the Sheiling. Heather would go with Alice and Charlie and John with the major and Jeremy.

1. assourdissant
2. joua
3. boutons
4. chant funèbre en gaélique
5. encore plus coupée
6. les Lady Jane de ce monde
7. autrefois
8. chouette
9. qu'elles dépassent
10. signalant au monde entier
11. carrière désaffectée
12. au nez crochu
13. capot
14. les répartit en groupes de deux
15. vive

Alice fished diligently until Heather announced they should break for lunch. Fishing fever had her in its grip and she had not thought of Jeremy once.

At lunch it transpired[1] that Lady Jane and the major were missing[2]. Jeremy said the local ghillie from Lochdubh had taken him aside and begun talking to him, and the major had packed up and left with him. Daphne said crossly that Lady Jane had thrashed her line about the water enough to scare away a whale[3] and then had mercifully[4] disappeared.

The absence of Lady Jane acted on the spirits[5] of the party[6] like champagne. Heather had augmented the hotel lunch with homemade sausage rolls, potato scones, and fruit bread covered in lashings[7] of butter and strawberry jam. Alice was dreamily happy to see that Daphne's skin was turning an ugly red in the sun while her own was turning to pale gold. A little breeze fanned their hot cheeks and Jeremy made Alice's day perfect by opting[8] to fish with her for the rest of the afternoon.

After some time, Jeremy suggested they should take a rest. Alice lay back on the springy heather by the water's edge and stared dreamily up into the blue sky.

'What do you think of Lady Jane?' asked Jeremy abruptly. Alice propped herself up[9] on one elbow. 'I dunno,' she said cautiously. 'I think she's learned the knack of fishing of a different sort[10]. I think she knows everyone's got some sort of skeleton in the cupboard[11] and she throws out remarks at random[12] and watches until she sees she's caught someone. Like with you and Daphne this morning. Whatever she meant by that ser-

1. Il s'avéra
2. avaient disparu
3. avait tellement agité sa ligne dans l'eau qu'elle aurait fait fuir une baleine
4. fort heureusement
5. humeur
6. groupe
7. d'une montagne
8. en choisissant
9. se redressa
10. qu'elle maîtrise un autre genre de pêche
11. un cadavre dans le placard
12. au hasard

vant and Spanish waiter remark, it upset you and Daphne no end[1].'

'Nonsense,' said Jeremy quickly. 'I was upset for Daphne's sake[2]. I could see the remark had got home[3].' But you were upset *before*, thought Alice. 'I think the woman's plain mad[4]. All that talk about her having power is pure rot[5]. She's nothing but the widow of some obscure Labour peer. She's not even good class[6]. I phoned my father about her the other night. He says she's the daughter of old Marie Phipps, who was secretary to and mistress of Lord Chalcont, and Marie forced his lordship into sending Jane to a finishing[7] school in Switzerland. There never was a Mr Phipps, you know.'

'You mean, she's *illegitimate*,' gasped[8] Alice. 'How splendid. I'd like to throw that in her face.'

'Don't, for God's sake,' said Jeremy harshly. 'She'd bite back like a viper.'

'But you said she's got no power.'

'Hasn't any power,' corrected Jeremy automatically, and Alice hated him for that brief moment. 'It's just that I'm thinking of standing for Parliament[9] and I'm very careful about avoiding enemies.'

'You'd be marvellous,' breathed[10] Alice. Why, he[11] could be Prime Minister! Maggie Thatcher couldn't live forever.

'You're a funny, intense little thing,' said Jeremy. He leaned forward and kissed her on the lips, a firm but schoolboyish[12] embrace. 'Now, let's go fish.' He grinned.

Alice waded dizzily[13] into the Sheiling, her legs trembling, a sick feeling[14] of excitement churning in her[15] stomach. The future Prime Minister of Britain had just kissed her! 'No comment,' she said to

1. vous l'avez tous les deux terriblement mal pris
2. pour Daphné
3. avait fait mouche
4. complètement folle
5. de la blague
6. même pas vraiment de la haute
7. [enseignant les bonnes manières aux jeunes filles]
8. hoqueta
9. à me présenter aux législatives
10. souffla
11. Mais oui, c'est qu'il
12. potache
13. tout étourdie
14. nausée
15. lui remuant l'

the clamouring press[1] as she swept[2] into Number Ten[3]. Where did Princess Di get her hats? She must find out.

Sunshine, physical exercise, and dreams of glory. Alice was often to look back on[4] that afternoon as the last golden period of her existence.

The sun burned down behind the mountains, making them two-dimensional cardboard mountains from a stage set[5]. The clear air was scented with thyme and sage[6] and pine.

To Alice's joy, Daphne had been suffering from mild sunstroke[7] and had been taken back to the hotel by Heather. So she was allowed to ride home with Jeremy.

There is nothing more sensuous than a rich fast car driven by a rich slow man through a Highland evening.

Alice felt languorous and sexy. The setting sun flashed between the trees and bushes as they drove along with the pale gold brilliance of the far north.

The grass was so very green[8] in this evening light, this gloaming[9]. Green as the fairy stories, green and gold as Never-Never Land[10]. Alice could well understand now why the Highlanders believed in fairies[11]. Jeremy slowed the car outside the village as the tall blonde Alice[12] had seen with Constable Macbeth came striding along the side of the road with two Irish wolfhounds[13] on the leash[14].

'That's the love of Constable Macbeth's life,' said Alice, delighted to have a piece of gossip[15].

'No hope there,' said Jeremy, cheerfully and unconsciously quoting Lady Jane. 'That's Priscilla Halburton-Smythe, daughter of Colonel James Halburton-Smythe. Her photograph was in

1. journalistes déchaînés
2. s'engouffrait
3. [résidence du Premier Ministre au Royaume-Uni]
4. repenserait souvent à
5. décor de théâtre
6. de sauge
7. d'une légère insolation
8. d'un vert si vif
9. crépuscule
10. le Pays imaginaire
11. aux fées
12. qu'Alice
13. lévriers irlandais
14. en laisse
15. potin

Country Life the other week. The Halburton-Smythes own most of the land around here.'

'Oh,' said Alice, feeling a certain kinship[1] with the village constable. 'Perhaps she loves him too.'

'She wouldn't be so silly,' said Jeremy. '*I* wouldn't even have a chance there.'

'Do people's backgrounds[2] matter a great deal to[3] you?' asked Alice in a low voice.

Jeremy reminded himself of his future as a politician. 'No,' he said stoutly[4]. 'I think all that sort of thing is rot[5]. A lady is a lady no matter what her background.'

Alice gave him a brilliant smile, and he smiled back, thinking she really was a very pretty little thing[6].

The sun disappeared as they plunged down to Lochdubh. Alice prayed that Jeremy would stop the car and kiss her again, but he seemed to have become immersed in his own thoughts.

When they arrived at the hotel, it was to find the rest of the fishing party surrounding Major Peter Frame. He was proudly holding up a large salmon while Heather took his photograph. Two more giants lay in plastic bags on the ground at his feet.

'How on earth did you do it?' said Jeremy, slapping the major on the back. 'Hey, that fellow's got a chunk[7] out the side.'

''Fraid[8] that's where I wrenched the hook out[9], old man,' said the major. 'Got too excited.' 'Gosh, I wish I had stayed with you,' said Jeremy. 'But I thought you went off somewhere else. Did you?'

The major laid his finger alongside his nose. 'Mum's the word[10], and talking about mum[11], the filthy Iron Curtain champers is on me[12] tonight.' 'Let's take them to the scales[13] and log[14] your

1. solidarité
2. les origines sociales
3. ont beaucoup d'importance pour
4. fermement
5. tout ça ne vaut pas un clou
6. mignonne comme tout
7. trou
8. [I'm afraid]
9. j'ai arraché le hameçon
10. Pas un mot à la reine mère
11. [sonne comme *Mumm*, une marque de champagne]
12. c'est ma tournée de champ' soviétique imbuvable
13. la balance
14. enregistrons

catch in the book,' said John, his face radiant[1]. The photograph would go to the local papers and the fishing magazines. He loved it when one of his pupils made a good catch. And no one had ever had such luck as this before.

They all were now looking forward to the evening, reminding themselves[2] that that was the time when Lady Jane could be guaranteed to be at her best[3]. They were to meet in the bar at eight to toast[4] the major's catch.

Alice slaved over[5] her appearance. She had bought one good dinner gown at an elegant Help the Aged[6] shop in Mayfair. Although the clothes were secondhand, most of them had barely been worn and the dinner gown was as good as new[7]. It was made of black silk velvet, very severe, cut low[8] in the front and slit up to mid-thigh[9] on either side of the narrow skirt.

She was ready at last, half an hour too early. This was one time Alice was determined to make an appearance[10]. Her high-heeled black sandals with thin straps[11] gave her extra[12] height and extra confidence. In the shaded light of the hotel room, her reflection looked poised and sophisticated.

Alice was just turning away from the mirror when all the barbed[13] remarks Lady Jane had made seemed to clamour[14] in her brain. It was no use pretending otherwise[15]; Lady Jane had set out to find out something about each one of them. Jeremy must never know[16]. The future Prime Minister of Britain could not have a wife with a criminal record[17]. But then, Lady Jane knew something about Jeremy. Had he seduced a servant? But that was an upper-class sin[18] and therefore forgivable[19], thought Alice miserably. She sat down on

1. radieux
2. tout en se rappelant
3. au mieux de sa forme
4. pour trinquer à
5. soigna laborieusement
6. [enseigne caritative d'articles de seconde main]
7. comme neuve
8. très décolleté
9. fendue jusqu'à mi-cuisse
10. entrée remarquée
11. brides
12. supplémentaire
13. cinglantes
14. retentir
15. inutile de prétendre le contraire
16. ne devait jamais l'apprendre
17. casier judiciaire
18. péché de la haute société
19. donc admissible

the edge of the bed and looked about her with bleak eyes[1].

How perfectly splendid it would be to go back to Mr Patterson-James and hand in her notice[2], and say she was going to be married to Jeremy Blythe – 'one of the Somerset Blythes, you know.' There was Mum and Dad in Liverpool to cope with[3]. Alice thought of her small, poky[4], shabby[5], comfortable home. Jeremy must never be allowed to go there. Mum and Dad would just have to travel to London for the wedding.

But between Alice and all those dreams stood Lady Jane. A wave of hate for Jane Winters engulfed Alice; primitive, naked hate.

Ten past eight! Alice leapt to her feet with an anguished look at her travel alarm.

The bar was crowded when she made her entrance. 'Dear me[6], the Merry Widow[7],' remarked Lady Jane, casting a pale look over Alice's black velvet gown. The fishing party had taken a table by the window where the major was cheerfully dispensing champagne. Alice's entrance had fallen flat because the major was describing how he had landed[8] his first salmon, and everyone was hanging on his every word[9]. 'It's almost a good enough story to be true[10],' said Lady Jane.

'Well, obviously it's true,' said the major, his good humour unimpaired[11]. 'Here I am and there are my fish, all waiting in the hotel freezer to be smoked. By the way, Alice, your trout's still there. You forgot to have it for breakfast.'

'You and Alice have a lot in common,' said Lady Jane sweetly. 'I can see that by the end of the week that hotel freezer will be *packed* with[12] fish that neither of you caught[13].'

1. d'un air sombre
2. lui donner sa démission
3. à affronter
4. riquiqui
5. miteux
6. Juste ciel
7. Veuve joyeuse
8. chopé
9. buvait ses paroles
10. assez beau pour être vrai
11. inentamée
12. bourré de
13. qu'aucun de vous n'a pêché

The rest of the group tried to ignore Lady Jane's remark. 'Tell us where exactly you caught those salmon, Major,' asked Jeremy.

'Yes, do tell,' echoed Daphne. 'It isn't fair to keep such a prize place to yourself[1].'

The major laughed and shook his head. 'Oh, *I'll* tell you,' said Lady Jane. She was wearing a sort of flowered pyjama suit[2] of the type that used to be in vogue in the thirties. Vermillion lipstick accentuated the petulant droop of her mouth[3]. 'I was talking to Ian Morrison, the ghillie, a little while ago and the dear man was in his cups[4] and told me *exactly* how you caught them.'

An awful silence fell on the group. The major stood with a bottle of champagne in one hand and a glass in the other and a silly smile pasted[5] on his face.

'I think we should go in to dinner,' said Heather loudly and clearly.

'I say, yes, let's[6],' said the major eagerly[7].

They all rose to their feet. Lady Jane remained seated, a gilt[8] sandal swinging from one plump foot as she looked up at them.

'Major Frame didn't catch those fish at all,' she said with hideous clarity. 'Ian Morrison took him up to the high pools on the Anstey. In one of those pools, three salmon had been trapped because of the river dwindling[9] suddenly in the heat. They were dying from lack of oxygen. One was half out of the water and a seagull[10] had torn a gash in its side[11], *not* the dear major's fictitious hook!'

One by one they filed into the dining room, not looking at each other, not looking at the major. Alice couldn't bear it any longer. She took a seat by the major. 'I don't believe a word of it,' she said,

1. garder pour vous un tel emplacement
2. costume
3. sa moue irritée
4. saoul
5. plaqué
6. allons-y
7. avec empressement
8. dorée
9. le fleuve s'est asséché
10. mouette
11. lui avait entaillé le flanc

patting[1] his hand. 'That terrible woman made it all up[2].'

The major smiled at her in a rigid sort of way and drank steadily from his champagne glass.

Charlie Baxter had been invited to join them for dinner. He had not been in the bar and therefore did not know about the major's humiliation. But he looked from face to face and then settled down to[3] eat his food so that he could escape as quickly as possible.

Lady Jane launched[4] into her usual evening flow of anecdotes while the rest stared at her[5] with hate-filled eyes.

What the major had done was not so bad[6]. Alice thought he had been very clever. She herself, she was sure, would have sworn blind[7] she had caught them.

Heather Cartwright was miserable[8]. She had already posted off the photographs, developed quickly by John in their own darkroom[9], to the local papers and fishing magazines. Heather didn't know which one she wanted to kill – Lady Jane or the major. When it had seemed as if the major had landed that splendid catch, Heather and John had heaved a sigh of relief[10]. Surely nothing Lady Jane said could touch them now. It was the most marvellous piece of publicity for the fishing school. But the silly, vain major had now played right into Lady Jane's hands[11]. Well *I* can just about bear it[12], thought Heather, but if anything happens to this fishing school, it will kill John.

'I always think those silly beanpole women[13] who model clothes[14] are a hoot[15],' Lady Jane was saying. 'I remember going to Hartnell's collection and there were the usual pan-faced[16] lot of mannequins modelling clothes for the Season and the

1. en tapotant
2. a tout inventé
3. se mit à
4. se lança
5. la fixaient
6. grave
7. juré ses grands dieux
8. très abattue
9. chambre noire
10. poussé un soupir de soulagement
11. s'était mis tout seul dans la gueule du loup
12. tout juste le supporter
13. grandes asperges
14. sont mannequins
15. hilarantes
16. impassibles

salon was so hot and stuffy and we were all half asleep. They were marching on saying in those awful sort of Putney[1] deb[2] voices, "For Goodwood, For Ascot[3]", and things like that, and then this one marches on and says, "For Cowes[4]", and we all laughed fit to burst[5].' Lady Jane herself laughed in a fat, jolly way.

Marvin Roth was gloomily longing for[6] the appearance of that village constable with the red hair. No one else seemed to have the courage to be rude to Lady Jane. If she did know something about him, Marvin Roth, then good luck to her. But that remark of hers to the constable about 'having power' was worrying. What sort of power?

Blackmail[7], thought Marvin Roth suddenly. That's it. And there was nothing he could do about it. Had they been in New York, then things might have been different. There was always someone who could be hired[8] to clear away[9] people like Lady Jane ... although he had heard that even in old New York things were not what they were in the early seventies, say[10], when a thousand dollars to the local Mafia could get someone wasted[11]. If only he could do it himself. Maybe he should just try to pay her off[12] before she approached him. Amy must never know. Amy was the prize[13]. In order to get divorced from that little whore of a first wife[14], he had paid an arm and a leg[15], but gaining Amy Blanchard had been worth it. He knew Amy hoped he would make it big[16] on the political scene. Of course, Amy either knew or had guessed about his unsavoury[17] past, but any approach to Lady Jane must be kept secret. There was a vein of steel running through Amy, and he was sure she would despise him[18] for trying to conciliate Lady Jane.

1. [quartier chic au sud de Londres, d'où part la régate Oxford contre Cambridge]
2. de débutantes
3. [marques de vêtements]
4. [sonne comme « vaches »]
5. étions toutes écroulées de rire
6. espérait sombrement
7. Du chantage
8. embauché
9. pour liquider
10. par exemple
11. faire descendre quelqu'un
12. de la soudoyer
13. récompense
14. de sa première femme, cette petite pute
15. la peau des fesses
16. allait réussir
17. douteux
18. le mépriserait

Marvin polished his bald head with his hand and looked sideways at Lady Jane. No ma'am, he thought, the day I let a broad like you screw up my act[1], well, you can kiss my ass[2] in Macy's window[3].

1. où je me laisserai emmerder par une gonzesse dans ton genre
2. compte là-dessus et va te faire voir
3. aux Galeries Lafayette

At last the horrible dinner was over. Alice smoothed down the velvet of her gown with a nervous hand and smiled hopefully at Jeremy. He looked at her vaguely and turned abruptly to Daphne Gore. 'Come on,' he said to Daphne. 'We've got to talk.'

Alice's eyes filmed over with[4] tears. She was dreadfully tired. She felt alien[5], foreign[6], alone. When she passed the bar, it was full of people drinking and laughing, the other guests who did not belong to the fishing school. She hesitated, longing for the courage to go in and join them, longing for just one compliment on her gown to make some of her misery go away.

4. se voilèrent de
5. exclue
6. étrangère

Constable Hamish Macbeth leaned on his garden gate and gazed across the loch to the lights of the hotel. He had fed the chickens and geese; his dog lay at his feet, stretched across his boots like a carriage rug[7], snoring peacefully.

7. couverture de voyage

Hamish lit a cigarette and pushed his cap back on his head. He was not happy, which was a fairly unusual state of mind for him. This was usually the time of the day he liked best.

He had to admit to himself he had let Lady Jane get under his skin[8]. He did not like the idea of that fat woman ferreting out[9] details of his family life, even if there was nothing shameful[10] to ferret out.

8. l'atteindre
9. déterrant
10. de honteux

It was true that Hamish Macbeth had six brothers and sisters to support[11]. He had been born one year after his parents had been married.

11. à entretenir

1. allait de soi
2. jusqu'à ce que le reste de la fratrie
3. de talent
4. braconnier
5. gibier
6. la fermette
7. peu d'argent que rapportaient les œufs de ses poules
8. prime
9. coureur en montagne
10. de suite
11. fermier
12. gentiment et de bonne grâce
13. ces derniers temps
14. la paroisse
15. se résumait
16. querelles
17. arrangées à l'amiable
18. pour ainsi dire
19. ne subissait pas
20. lotissement
21. projets
22. cas sociaux
23. arrachés
24. au confort bruyant des taudis urbains

After that there had been a long gap and then Mr and Mrs Macbeth had produced three boys and three girls in as quick a succession as was physically possible. As in many Celtic families, it was taken for granted[1] that the eldest son would remain a bachelor until such time as the next in line[2] were able to support themselves. Hamish had deliberately chosen the unambitious career of village constable because it enabled him to send most of his pay home. He was a skilful[3] poacher[4] and presents of venison[5] and salmon found their way regularly to his parents' croft[6] in Ross and Cromarty. The little egg money he got from his poultry[7] was sent home as well. Then there was the annual prize money[8] for best hill runner[9] at the Strathbane Highland games. Hamish had taken the prize five years in a row[10].

His father was a crofter[11] but could not make nearly enough to support all six younger children. Hamish had accepted his lot as he accepted most things, with easy-going good nature[12].

But of late[13], he had found himself wishing he had a little bit more money in his pocket and yet he would not admit to himself the reason for this.

What he *could* admit to himself was that he was very worried about the fishing class. Crime in Hamish's parish[14] usually ran[15] to things like bigamy or the occasional drunk on a Saturday night. Most village wrangles[16] were settled out of court[17], so to speak[18], by the diplomatic Hamish. He was not plagued with[19] the savage violence of poaching gangs, although he felt sure that would come. A new housing estate[20] was being built outside the village; one of those mad schemes[21] where the worst of the welfare cases[22] were wrenched[23] out of the cosy clamour of the city slums[24] and transported to the awesome bleakness[1] of the Highlands. To Hamish, these housing estates were the breeding grounds[2] of poaching gangs who dynamited the salmon to the surface and fought each other with razors and sharpened[3] bicycle chains.

Something in his bones seemed to tell him that trouble was going to come from this fishing class. He decided it was time to find out a little more about Lady Jane.

He sifted through[4] the filing cabinet of his mind[5], which was filled with the names and addresses and telephone numbers of various friends and relatives[6]. Like most Highlanders, Hamish had relatives scattered all over[7] the world.

Then he remembered his second[8] cousin, Rory Grant, who worked for the *Daily Recorder* in Fleet Street[9]. Hamish ambled indoors[10] and put through a collect call[11]. 'This is Constable Macbeth of Lochdubh with a verra[12] important story for Rory Grant,' said Hamish when the newspaper switchboard[13] showed signs of being reluctant[14] to pay for the call. When he was at last put through to Rory, Hamish gave a description of Lady Jane Winters and asked for details about her.

'I'll need to go through to the library and look at her cuttings[15],' said Rory. 'It might take a bit of time. I'll call you back.'

'Och, no,' said Hamish comfortably, 'I am not paying for the call, so I will just hold on and have a beer while you are looking.'

'Suit yourself[16],' said Rory. Hamish tucked[17] the phone under one ear and fished a bottle of beer out of his bottom drawer[18]. He did not like cold beer and, in any case, Hamish had grown up on[19] American movies where the hero had fished[20] a bottle out of his desk drawer, and had never got over[21]

1. imposante désolation
2. terreau fertile
3. affûtées
4. parcourut
5. son classeur mental
6. parents à lui
7. un peu partout dans
8. issu de germain
9. [rue des grands journaux britanniques, à Londres]
10. rentra [chez lui] d'un pas tranquille
11. passa un appel en PCV
12. [very]
13. standard
14. réticence
15. coupures de presse
16. Comme tu voudras
17. cala
18. tiroir
19. été élevé aux
20. sorti
21. ne s'était jamais lassé

the thrill[1] of being able to do the same thing, even though it was warm beer and not bourbon.

He had left the police office door open, and a curious hen[2] came hopping in, flew up on top of the typewriter, and stared at him with curious, beady eyes[3].

Priscilla Halburton-Smythe suddenly appeared in the doorway, a brace of grouse[4] dangling from one hand[5], and smiled at the sight of Hamish with his huge boots on the desk, bottle of beer in one hand, phone in the other and hen in front.

'I see you're interviewing one of the village criminals,' said Priscilla.

'Not I,' said Hamish. 'I am waiting for my cousin in London to come back to the telephone with some vital information.'

'I meant the hen, silly. Joke. I've brought you some grouse.'

'Have they been hung?'

'No, I shot them today. Why do you ask?'

'Oh, nothing, nothing. It is verra kind of you, Miss Halburton-Smythe.'

Since Hamish's family did not like grouse, the policeman was calculating how soon he could manage to get into Ullapool, where he would no doubt get a good price for the brace from one of the butchers. If they were fresh, that would give him a few days. Hamish did not possess a freezer except the small compartment in his refrigerator, which was full of TV dinners[6].

Hamish stood up, startling[7] the hen, who flew off with a squawk[8], and pulled out a chair for Priscilla. He studied her as she sat down. She was wearing a beige silk blouse tucked into cord breeches[9]. Her waist was small and her breasts high and firm. The pale oval of her face, framed

1. du frisson
2. poule
3. petits yeux perçants
4. avec deux oies sauvages [d'Écosse]
5. qui lui pendaient de la main
6. plats tout faits
7. effarouchant
8. en couinant
9. un pantalon de velours côtelé

by the pale gold of her hair, was saved from being insipid by a pair of bright blue eyes fringed with[1] sooty[2] lashes. He cleared his throat. 'I cannot leave the telephone. But you will find a bottle of beer in the refrigerator in the kitchen.'

'I thought you didn't like cold beer,' called Priscilla over her shoulder as she made her way across the tiny hall to the kitchen. 'I aye[3] keep one for the guests,' called Hamish, thinking wistfully[4] that he had kept a cold bottle of beer especially for her since that golden day she had first dropped in[5] to see him about a minor poaching matter four whole months ago. 'No more trouble, I hope,' added Hamish as Priscilla returned with a foaming glass. 'I hope it is not the crime that brings you here.'

'No, I thought you might like some birds for the pot[6].' Priscilla leaned back and crossed her legs, tightening the material[7] along her thighs by the movement. Hamish half closed his eyes. 'Actually[8], I'm escaping,' said Priscilla. 'Daddy's brought the most awful twit[9] up from London. He wants me to marry him.'

'And will you?'

'No, you silly constable. Didn't I just say he was a twit? I say, there's a picture show[10] on at the village hall[11] tonight. Second showing[12], ten o'clock. Wouldn't it be a shriek[13] if we went to it?'

Hamish smiled. 'My dear lassie[14], it is Bill Haley and his Comets in *Rock Around the Clock*, which was showing[15] a wee bit[16] before you were born, I'm thinking.'

'Lovely. Let's go after whoever you're speaking to speaks.'

1. ourlés de
2. noirs
3. toujours
4. avec mélancolie
5. ce jour béni où elle avait débarqué
6. marmite
7. tissu
8. En fait
9. pire crétin
10. projection
11. mairie
12. séance
13. super
14. demoiselle [écossais]
15. était déjà sorti
16. un petit bout de temps

'I cannot think Colonel Halburton-Smythe would like his daughter to go to the pictures with the local bobby[1].'

'He won't know.'

'You have not been long in the Highlands. Give it a day[2], give it a week, everyone around here knows everything.'

'But Daddy doesn't *speak* to anyone in the village.'

'Your housemaid, Maisie, is picture daft[3]. She'll be there. She'll tell the other servants and that po-faced[4] butler[5], Jenkins, will see it as his duty to inform the master.'

'Do you care[6]?'

'Not much,' grinned Hamish. 'Oh, Rory, it is yourself.'

He listened intently. Priscilla watched Hamish's face, noticing for the first time how cat-like his hazel eyes looked[7] with their Celtic narrowness at the outer edges[8].

'Thank you, Rory,' said Hamish finally. 'That is verra interesting. I am surprised that fact about her is not better known.'

The voice quacked[9] again.

'Thank you,' said Hamish gloomily. 'I may be in the way of having to[10] report a wee[11] murder to you in the next few days. No, it is chust[12] my joke, Rory.' Hamish's accent became more sibilant[13] and Highland when he was seriously upset[14].

He put down the phone and stared into space.

'What was all that about?' asked Priscilla curiously.

'Gossip[15] about a gossip[16],' said Hamish, getting to his feet. 'Wait and I'll just lock up, Miss Halburton-Smythe, and we'll be on our way. I'll tell you about it one of these days.'

1. flic du coin
2. Au bout d'une journée
3. dingue de ciné
4. imperturbable
5. maître d'hôtel
6. Vous vous en souciez
7. l'air félin de ses yeux noisette
8. bords écossais très étroits
9. nasilla
10. Il se pourrait que je doive
11. petit
12. [just]
13. sifflant
14. très ému
15. Des commérages
16. commère

Day Four

Above all, when playing[1] a big fish, stay calm.
– Peter Wheat, *The Observer's Book of Fly Fishing*

1. vous êtes aux prises avec

It was a very subdued[2] party that met in the lounge in the morning. Heather Cartwright was visibly losing her usual phlegmatic calm. Her plump face was creased with[3] worry, and her voice shook as she asked them to be seated.

2. morose
3. ridé par

Lady Jane was absent, but everyone seemed to jump[4] a little when anyone entered the room. John Cartwright, in a weary voice[5], said he felt they had not all learnt the art of casting properly and so he would take them out to the lawn at the back to give a demonstration. His eyes turned to the major to make his usual remark, that those with experience could go ahead[6], but somehow he could not bring himself to say anything.

4. sursauter
5. d'un ton las
6. partir de leur côté

They stood about him, shivering in the chill, misty morning air as he demonstrated how to make the perfect cast. He warmed to[7] his subject but his little audience[8] fidgetted restlessly[9] and moved from foot to foot.

7. s'enthousiasmait pour
8. public
9. gigotait sans arrêt

Finally, their unease reached him, and he stopped his lecture with a little sigh. 'Enough from me,' he said. 'We will go to the upper reaches of the river Anstey. I'll leave word at the desk[10]

10. réception

for Lady Jane. There is no point in[1] disturbing her if she's sleeping late.'

Like the day before, the warmth of the sun began to penetrate the mist. 'Bad day for fishing,' said the major knowledgeably[2], and Alice could only envy the quick way in which he had recovered from his humiliation.

'I like the sunshine,' she said, and then could not resist adding, 'and I hope Lady Jane doesn't turn up to spoil it.'

'Got a feeling[3] we won't be seeing her,' said the major cheerfully.

And then it was as if they all had the same feeling. Everyone's spirits[4] began to lift. John Cartwright smiled at his wife and pressed her hand as he drove up the twists and winds[5] to the river. 'I've a feeling we've been worrying too much about that woman,' he murmured to Heather. 'Don't worry. I'll see to it[6] she doesn't plague us anymore[7].'

Alice gave a little sigh of relief. Obviously the Cartwrights were going to tell Lady Jane to leave. She grinned at Charlie, but Charlie was looking white and sick and turned his head away.

She shrugged. Again, the sunshine was bleaching away[8] the worries of the night. She was prepared to accept that she did not stand a chance with Jeremy. Let him have Daphne. There was no use fighting it. She would enjoy the exercise and scenery as much as she could. Once more her thoughts returned to Mr Patterson-James. She was sure he would be impressed when she described her holiday.

But when she climbed out of the car and waited for Heather to hand her her rod, she could

1. Inutile de
2. d'un ton docte
3. l'impression
4. L'humeur
5. la route sinueuse
6. vais veiller à ce qu'
7. ne nous ennuie plus
8. effaçait

not help wishing Jeremy would join her as he had done on the other days.

But John Cartwright, with the continued absence of Lady Jane, was once more on form. He was determined his little class should get the proper schooling[1]. He said he was going to give them a demonstration of how to catch a salmon. When they all had their gear on[2] he led the way up a twisting path beside the river at a smart trot[3]. Alice felt the sweat beginning to trickle down her face as she stumbled along after him. Below them, at the bottom of the steep bank, the river Anstey foamed and frothed[4]. At times, delicate strands of silver birch[5] and alder[6] and hazel[7] screened the river from their view[8], and then, around another turn it would appear again, tumbling headlong on its way to the sea. To the right, the tangled[9] forest climbed up the mountainside.

Marvin Roth put an arm around his wife's shoulders to help her. 'Didn't mean to take you on a survival course[10],' he said. Amy shook his arm away and strode ahead of him up the path with long, athletic strides[11]. Marvin hesitated, took off his cap, and passed a hand over the dome of his bald head. Then he replaced his cap and plunged[12] after her.

'What's up with you[13] this morning, Miss Alice?' came Jeremy's voice behind Alice. 'Don't I get a smile?'

Remember, it's no use, Alice chided herself[14] fiercely[15]. Aloud she said, 'I haven't any energy to do anything other than try to keep up[16]. It's so *hot*. I didn't think the Scottish Highlands would be so hot.'

'It's like this sometimes,' said Jeremy, falling into step beside her[17]. He was wearing a blue cotton

1. groupe soit formé comme il convenait
2. eurent tous enfilé leur équipement,
3. à vive allure
4. écumait
5. bouleaux blancs
6. d'aulnes
7. de noisetiers
8. masquaient le cours d'eau
9. enchevêtrée
10. parcours du combattant
11. enjambées
12. se lança
13. Qu'est-ce qui vous arrive
14. se tança
15. vertement
16. de suivre
17. en venant marcher à ses côtés

shirt open at the neck, as blue as the sky above. He smelled of clean linen[1], aftershave, and masculine sweat. The heavy gold band of his wrist watch lay against[2] the brand-new tan[3] of his arm. Alice's good resolutions began to fade[4].

'What did you think about our major's little trick[5]?' Jeremy went on. 'Not quite the manner of the officer or the gentleman, as our Lady Jane would point out[6].'

'I think it was understandable,' said Alice. 'It must have been a terrible temptation to lie. Only think the way people go on about cars and horses and ... boats. It's surely more in the nature of a gentleman to *lie* when it comes to sports.'

She gave Jeremy a rather hard-eyed stare[7]. Alice's better nature was trying to drive him away[8], but Jeremy only felt she had gone off him[9] and was a little piqued[10].

'Didn't *you* lie yourself?' he jeered[11]. 'Our gossip accused you of lying about the fish you were *supposed* to have caught.'

Easy tears rushed to Alice's eyes. 'I think you're horrid. How can you accuse me of such a thing?'

'Hey, steady on[12]!' Jeremy caught her arm. 'There's no need to fly off the handle[13] like that.'

'I don't know what's up with me[14],' said Alice, scrubbing her eyes with the back of her hand. 'I think it's that Jane female. She's always hinting things[15] in a spiteful sort of way.' 'You know,' said Jeremy, taking Alice's hand in a warm clasp. 'I don't think we'll ever see her again. I feel she's taken the hint[16] and left. No one can be that thick-skinned[17] – it surely got through to her[18] that not one of us can stand her[19].'

He gave her hand a squeeze. Alice's mercurial spirits soared[20], and her resolution to forget about

1. linge
2. tranchait sur
3. tout nouveau bronzage
4. à faiblir
5. ruse
6. le ferait remarquer
7. regard assez dur
8. l'éconduire
9. qu'il ne lui plaisait plus
10. vexé
11. railla-t-il
12. doucement
13. de prendre la mouche
14. ce que j'ai
15. à insinuer des trucs
16. a compris
17. insensible à ce point
18. elle a sûrement capté
19. la supporter
20. L'humeur inconstante d'Alice revint au beau fixe

Jeremy whirled up[1] to the summer sky and disappeared. After they had been climbing about a mile, and Amy Roth was loudly and clearly threatening to call it a day[2] and turn back, John finally came to a stop. 'Down here to the Keeper's Pool,' he called, 'and be very quiet.' The tangled undergrowth[3] gave way[4] at their side of the pool where a ledge of flat rocks hung over[5] the water. The pool swirled and boiled like a witch's cauldron[6].

It was a joy to watch John casting. He did a roll cast[7] across the pool, landing the fly delicately on the surface. All at once, fishing fever gripped John and he forgot about his class. Suddenly, with a flash of silver scales[8], a salmon leapt high in the air. Alice clapped her hands in excitement, and everyone said, 'Shhhhh.[9]'

Now the whole class was as intense as their teacher. Then, just as John was casting, Charlie slipped and nearly fell into the pool. Heather shouted, 'Look out[10]!' and caught his arm. John turned to make sure the boy was safe, leaving his line tumbling and turning in the water.

He turned back once he had assured himself that Charlie was all right. He flicked at his line[11] and his rod began to bend. 'You've got one,' breathed[12] the major.

'I don't know ... I think it's a rock,' muttered John. He moved to another angle and tried to reel in[13] his line. He had something heavy on the end of it, something that was twisting and turning.

His heart began to beat hard. Of course, if it wasn't a rock, it could be a sunken[14] branch, twisting and turning in the churning of the water[15]. He moved back round to where the group was standing on the beach of rocks. Underneath the rock shelf

1. s'envola joyeusement
2. de tout arrêter
3. broussailles enchevêtrées
4. s'arrêtaient
5. corniche surplombait
6. le chaudron d'une sorcière
7. lancer roulé
8. écailles argentées
9. Chut !
10. Attention
11. fouetta sa ligne [d'un mouvement du poignet]
12. souffla
13. ramener [avec le moulinet]
14. coulée
15. remous

the water was clear and still, a little island of calm just outside the churning of the pool.

He reeled in again, feeling his excitement fade as whatever it was that he had hooked moved from the turbulent water into the still shallows[1]. A log[2], he thought.

And then Daphne Gore, the usually cool and unflappable[3] Daphne, began to scream and scream, harsh, terror-stricken screams tearing apart[4] the sylvan picture[5] of pretty woods, singing birds, and tumbling water.

Alice stared down into the golden water directly below her feet as she stood on the ledge. And Lady Jane stared back[6].

Slowly rising to the surface came the bloated[7], distorted[8] features[9] of Lady Jane Winters. Her tongue was sticking out[10], and her blue eyes bulged[11] and glared straight up into[12] the ring of faces.

'She must have hit her head and fallen in,' whispered Alice, clinging to Jeremy.

John waded into the water, heaved the body up[13], and then let it fall with a splash. He turned a chalk-white[14] face up to Heather. 'Get Macbeth,' he said. 'Get the police.'

'But didn't she just fall?' asked Heather, as white as her husband.

John prodded at[15] Lady Jane's fat neck. 'There's a leader[16] round her neck. She's been strangled. And look.' He pointed to Lady Jane's legs.

'Oh, God,' said Alice, 'there's chains wrapped round them.'

'She could have done it herself,' said Amy Roth through white lips. 'Marvin. Help me. I feel sick[17].'

1. calme des eaux peu profondes
2. bûche
3. imperturbable
4. qui ébranlèrent
5. cadre sylvestre
6. lui rendit son regard
7. bouffis
8. déformés
9. traits
10. Elle tirait la langue
11. saillaient
12. fixaient
13. souleva le corps
14. d'un blanc crayeux
15. désigna
16. bas de ligne
17. vais vomir

'Get the police, dammit,' shouted John. 'And get that child out of here. The rest, stay where you are.'

'If it's murder, we'd better all stay,' said Marvin, holding Amy tightly against him.

'Don't be silly,' said Heather. 'It took[1] someone powerful to overcome[2] a woman like Lady Jane and strangle her with a leader. Come along, Charlie. I'll take you to your aunt's and then I'll bring Constable Macbeth.'

'Take me to your leader[3],' said Daphne and began to giggle[4].

'Can't anyone stop her?' pleaded Amy.

'Pull yourself together[5], Daphne,' snapped[6] John Cartwright.

'Steady the buffs[7],' urged the major.

Daphne sat down abruptly, pulled out a gold cigarette case, and extracted a cigarette with hands that trembled so much the cigarettes spilled out[8] on the rock. Jeremy stooped[9] to help her. Their eyes met and held in a long stare.

'Go up the hill and wait at the top,' commanded John. 'I'll stay with the body.'

Alice, Jeremy, Daphne, the major, and Marvin and Amy Roth made their way up the path. They moved, bunched together[10], along the upper path until it opened out into a small glade[11]. They sat down in silence. Major Peter Frame pulled out a packet of cigarettes and offered them around.

Marvin was the first to speak. 'I always knew that dame[12] was a party pooper[13],' he said gloomily. 'She's worse dead than alive. She was murdered, of course.'

'Well, it wasn't any of us,' said Alice. She tried to speak bravely, but her voice trembled and she rubbed at the gooseflesh[14] on her arms.

1. a fallu
2. vaincre
3. Menez-moi à votre chef [jeu de mots avec le *bas de ligne*, arme du crime]
4. à rire nerveusement
5. Reprenez-vous
6. dit sèchement
7. Du calme dans les rangs
8. se renversèrent
9. se pencha
10. groupés comme un seul homme
11. clairière
12. que cette bonne femme
13. rabat-joie
14. chair de poule

'Yeah, she was the sort of woman *anyone* would have murdered, I reckon[1],' said Amy Roth shakily. 'Was she rich? Maybe one of her relatives followed her up here and bumped her off[2].'

'By Jove[3], I think you're right,' the major chimed in[4] eagerly[5]. 'I mean *de mortuis*[6] and all that, but she was a really repulsive, nasty woman. Look at the way she kept getting at each of us[7]. Stands to reason[8] she'd been doing the same thing to other people for years.'

'I suppose the holiday's over,' said Daphne, looking once more her calm self[9]. 'I mean, what's going to happen to us?'

'It won't be left to Macbeth, not a murder,' said Jeremy. 'They'll be sending in some of the big brass[10]. I s'pose they'll take statements from us[11], take a note of our home addresses, and let us go.'

'It's so unfair,' drawled[12] Daphne. 'Just as I was getting the hang[13] of this fishing thing. You know, I felt so sure that today would be the day I would catch something.'

Everyone looked at Daphne with approval. They were not only joined[14] by the tragedy of the murder but bound in fellowship[15] by that old-as-time obsession, the lure[16] of the kill.

'Well, I've paid for this week and I jolly well expect to get full value[17],' said the major, 'or they'll need to give me my money back. As soon as that oaf of a village copper[18] gets our statements, I'm off to spend the rest of the day fishing, and if John Cartwright isn't up to it[19], I'll take any of you as pupils[20] if you'll have me[21].'

'I'll go with you for a start,' said Jeremy, and the others nodded. The major might have lied about his magnificent salmon bag, but he was undoubtedly[22] an expert angler. His line never

1. à mon avis
2. l'a butée
3. Sacrebleu
4. renchérit
5. vivement
6. le respect dû aux morts
7. n'arrêtait pas de s'en prendre à chacun de nous
8. Logiquement,
9. qui paraissait avoir repris ses esprits
10. un grand chef
11. qu'on va prendre nos dépositions
12. dit d'un ton traînant
13. prenais le coup de main
14. liés
15. aussi unis
16. attrait
17. compte bien en avoir pour mon argent
18. abruti de flic de village
19. en mesure de le faire
20. élèves
21. si vous êtes d'accord
22. sans l'ombre d'un doute

became tangled in bushes, and he made his own flies, several of which flaunted their garish colours on[1] his hat.

'I thought of killing her,' said Alice suddenly. 'I'm *glad* she's dead, and I feel guilty at the same time. I feel I *wished* her to death.'

There was a shocked silence.

'Well,' said Jeremy uncomfortably, 'may as well be honest. I think we all felt like that.'

'Not me,' said Amy Roth. The skin at the corners of her eyelids had a stretched, almost oriental look. 'We Blanchards are made of pretty strong stuff[2].'

'Tell us about it,' said Daphne harshly[3]. 'Tell us about the bloody ol' plantation and massah's in de col', col' ground[4]. Tell us anything in the world, but don't talk about the murder.'

'Not if you're going to be rude[5],' said Amy, leaning against her husband's shoulder and seeking his hand for comfort.

'I didn't mean to be rude. I really would like to hear about it. All I can think of is a sort of *Gone With the Wind* setting[6], all crinolines and mint juleps[7].'

Amy laughed. 'Believe it or not, it was a little bit like that. Of course, that life all went[8] when I was still a child. Pa was a gambler[9] in the true Southern tradition. Well, lemme[10] see. It was a big barn of a place[11], the Blanchard mansion, like you see in the movies. Pillared colonial front, wide verandahs all round. Green shutters[12], cool rooms smelling of bees-wax and lavender. Flowers evvywheah[13],' said Amy, becoming Southern in accent as she warmed to her subject. Amy's normal voice was a light, almost Bostonian accent. 'And antiques! I decleah[14], there were more

1. ornaient de leurs couleurs vives
2. du genre solide
3. durement
4. [caricature d'accent afro-américain]
5. grossière
6. cadre à la *Autant en emporte le vent*
7. des cocktails bourbon-menthe
8. a complètement disparu
9. joueur
10. [let me]
11. espèce de grand hangar
12. Des volets
13. [everywhere]
14. [declare]

Chippendales[1] and whatyoucallums[2] there than you'd get in one of your English stately homes[3]. We hud[4] been importing them for yeahs[5].'

'Listen!' The major put a hand to his ear in a sort of list-who-approacheth way[6]. Most of his gestures were stagey[7].

Heather appeared with Constable Macbeth behind her. The policeman was wearing his usual black uniform, shiny with wear[8]. He pulled off his cap, and his red hair blazed[9] in the sun like fire. It was that true Highland red that sometimes looked as if it has purple lights.

'I will chust[10] go down and look at the body,' he said placidly. 'There will be detectives[11] coming up from Strathbane by this afternoon, but I must make sure nothing is touched. If you will wait where you are, I will return in a wee[12] moment and take the statements.'

They waited now in silence. A little knot of dread[13] was beginning to form in the pit of each stomach. It had just been becoming comfortably unreal. Now reality was with them in the shape of the village constable who was down at the pool bent over the body.

A small, fussy[14] man erupted[15] into the glade and glared about him[16]. 'Dr MacArthur,' said Heather, 'I'll take you down. Mr Macbeth is with the body now.'

'The procurator fiscal[17] is on his way from Strathbane,' said the doctor. 'But I may as well make a preliminary examination. Macbeth's talking about murder. But the man's havering[18]. She could have got her own leader wrapped around her neck and fallen into the pool.'

'And wrapped chains around her legs to sink her?' said Marvin Roth dryly.

1. [meubles du célèbre ébéniste du XVIIIe s.]
2. de trucs
3. vieux manoirs
4. [had]
5. [years]
6. en un geste mimant « qui va là ? »
7. théâtraux
8. d'usure
9. flamboyait
10. [just]
11. des gens de la PJ
12. petit
13. peur
14. agité
15. fit irruption dans
16. lança des regards furieux alentour
17. procureur [en Écosse]
18. c'est n'importe quoi [écossais]

'Eh, what? Better go and see.'

He disappeared with Heather.

Again, the group waited.

'I'm hungry,' said Alice at last. 'I know I shouldn't feel hungry, but I am. Would it be too awful if we went back to the cars and had something to eat?'

'Better wait,' said the major. 'Can't be very long now.'

But it seemed ages[1]. They could hear people coming and going. The sun was very high in the sky, and flies droned[2] and danced in the green quiet of the glade.

At last, Hamish Macbeth appeared looking hot and grim[3].

'We'll all just be going back to the hotel,' he said. 'I'm getting this path closed off[4] until the big brass arrives. The water bailiffs have said they will stand guard[5].'

A moment before, each one of them had felt he would give anything to be able to move. Now they were overcome by a strange reluctance[6]. There was one large fact each of them had to face up to[7] sooner or later, and each one was putting off[8] the moment.

They all gathered in the hotel lounge. Constable Macbeth surveyed them solemnly.

'The manager has given me the use of the wee room off[9] the reception, so I'll take you one at a time. You first, Mr Cartwright.'

'I'll come too,' said Heather quickly.

'No need for that,' said the constable easily[10]. 'This way, Mr Cartwright.'

Heather sat down, flushed with distress. She looked like a mother seeing her youngest off to boarding school[11] for the first time.

1. interminable
2. bourdonnaient
3. sombre
4. vais faire fermer ce chemin
5. monteront la garde
6. pris d'une étrange réticence
7. regarder en face
8. en repoussait
9. qui donne sur
10. tranquillement
11. accompagnant son petit dernier en pension

John followed Hamish Macbeth into a small, dark room furnished simply with a scarred[1] wooden desk, some old filing cabinets[2], and two hard chairs. Hamish sat down behind the desk, and John took the chair opposite.

1. éraflé
2. casiers à tiroirs

'Now,' said the policeman, producing a large notebook, 'we'll make a start. It is the doctor's guess that Lady Jane was in the water all night. When did you last see her?'

'At dinner last night,' said John. 'We were celebrating the major's catch[3].'

3. prise

'Or rather, the major's find[4],' murmured Hamish. 'And was she wearing then[5] what she was wearing when she was found dead?'

4. trouvaille
5. portait-elle alors

'Yes, I mean no. No, she was wearing a flowery trouser suit thing last night with evening sandals. She seemed to be wearing her usual fishing outfit[6] when ... when we saw her in the pool.'

6. tenue

Hamish made a note and then looked up. 'Did you know Lady Jane's job?'

'Job?' said John. 'I didn't know she worked.'

'Well, we'll leave that until later. Did your wife know the nature of Lady Jane's job, I wonder?'

A faint line of sweat glistened[7] on John's upper lip. There was a silence. Hamish patiently repeated the question.

7. brilla

'No,' said John, suddenly and savagely. 'Look here, Macbeth, what is this? You know us both. Do you think either of us would kill her?'

'That is not for me to say[8],' said Hamish. 'But I willnae[9] get to the person[10] who did it if I don't start to eliminate those that did not. Now what were you doing late last night?'

8. à moi de le dire
9. [will not]
10. mettre la main sur celui

'How late?'

'She was last seen going up to her room at ten-thirty, according to the hotel servants.'

'I went to bed,' said John, 'and Heather too. We'd had a fairly exhausting day.'

'Did anyone in the group seem to hate Lady Jane?'

'No, we all loved her,' said John sarcastically. 'Good God, man, use your wits[1]. Nobody liked her, not even you.'

'Mphmm. Lady Jane had a nasty habit[2] of making remarks. Did she say anything to you?'

'Nothing in particular. Just general carping[3].'

'Aye[4], well, that will do for now. If you'll just send Mrs Cartwright in.'

As John entered the room, Alice was saying with a nervous giggle, 'Just think. One of us must have killed her. I mean, it stands to reason[5] ...'

It was out in the open now, put into words; that thought they had been keeping resolutely at bay[6] since Lady Jane's body was discovered.

'He wants to see you,' said John to Heather. He added in a low voice as he held open the door for her, 'I told him we didn't know what she did.'

The door to the lounge opened, and a small, anxious-looking woman dressed in a lumpy[7], powder-blue dress fussed in, dragging[8] Charlie with her. 'I'm Mrs Baxter, Tina Baxter,' she announced, staring around the room with rather bulging[9] blue eyes. 'I only arrived today. My poor boy.' She tried to hug Charlie, but he flinched away from[10] this public demonstration of maternal affection.

'You should keep the boy away from this,' said John. 'There was no need to bring him along.'

'There was every need[11],' said Tina Baxter. 'I was told the police wanted to interrogate the whole fishing class and nobody is going to frighten my little boy with a lot of questions.' She proceeded to tell the bemused company[12] about

1. servez-vous de votre jugeote
2. la sale habitude
3. des chicaneries
4. Oui
5. c'est logique
6. à distance
7. boudinée
8. entra l'air agité, en traînant
9. exorbités
10. s'écarta, refusant
11. Bien au contraire
12. l'assistance médusée

her divorce and the difficulties of rearing[1] a boy single-handed[2], and that Charlie had written to her saying this Lady Jane was a cruel and evil woman. Her words began to tumble out one over the other[3] in an increasingly unintelligible stream[4].

Then she stopped suddenly and stared at the door with her mouth open. Hamish's big brass had arrived from Strathbane.

A big, heavyset man draped in a grey double-breasted suit[5] introduced himself as Detective Chief Inspector Blair. He was flanked by two other detectives, Jimmy Anderson and Harry MacNab. Jimmy Anderson was thin and wiry with suspicious blue eyes, and MacNab was short and dumpy[6] with thick black hair and wet-looking black eyes.

'Which one of you runs[7] this school?' demanded Mr Blair. He spoke with a thick Glaswegian[8] accent.

'I do,' said John. 'Constable Macbeth is talking to my wife at the moment.'

'Where?'

'In there,' said John. 'I'll show you the way.'

'No need,' said Blair. 'We'll introduce ourselves.'

Hamish got to his feet as the three men entered the small office. Heather gratefully escaped.

'Macbeth, is it?' said Blair, sitting down in the chair Hamish had just vacated. 'We've got a real juicy one[9] here. Bit out of your league[10], Constable. The boys and the forensic[11] team are combing the ground[12]. Good bit of work on your part to get the water bailiffs to stand guard.'

He smiled at Hamish and waited for a look of gratitude to appear on the constable's face at the compliment. Hamish looked stolidly[13] back, and Blair scowled[14] with irritation.

1. élever
2. toute seule
3. à se déverser
4. flot de plus en plus inintelligible
5. veston croisé
6. courtaud
7. dirige
8. de Glasgow
9. gros coup
10. Ça dépasse vos compétences
11. médico-légale
12. passent la zone au peigne fin
13. impassiblement
14. fronça les sourcils

'Yes, well, I suppose they all know they're supposed to stay put[1] until I'm satisfied[2] that no one in this school did it. School, indeed. All that money and fuss[3] just to catch a fish.'

'I think it would be better if I told them they are not to leave Lochdubh at the moment,' said Hamish. 'Them not having the ESP[4].'

'Enough of that,' snapped Blair. 'Before I have the rest in[5], what do you think the motive was for this murder?'

'I think it had something to do with Lady Jane's job,' said Hamish slowly.

'Job? What job?'

'Lady Jane Winters was, in fact, Jane Maxwell, columnist[6] for the London *Evening Star*.'

'That rag[7]! Well, what's so bad about being a columnist?'

'I understand she specialized in taking holidays where there were going to be small groups of British people. She would find out something nasty about each one, since she liked to prove that everyone has a skeleton in the closet. There have been complaints[8] to the press council[9], but her column's been too popular. Folks chust lap it up[10] and think it will never happen to them. Maybe someone in this group knew about her column, although the fact that she was Jane Maxwell was kept a closely guarded secret[11].'

'And how did *you* find out if it's that much of a[12] secret?' asked Blair, his eyes raking over[13] the lanky length of the village constable.

'I haff[14] my methods, Watson,' grinned Hamish.

'I am not putting up with any cheek[15] from a Highlander,' snarled Blair. 'How did you find out?'

'I have a relative that works in Fleet Street.'

1. ne pas bouger
2. sois sûr
3. tout ce tralala
4. Vu qu'ils sont pas devins [*not having extrasensory perception*]
5. que je fasse venir les autres
6. chroniqueuse
7. torchon
8. des plaintes
9. conseil déontologique de la presse
10. en raffolent
11. un secret bien gardé
12. un tel
13. balayant
14. [have]
15. ne vais pas supporter d'insolence

'And which of these fishing lot knew about her being Jane Maxwell?'

'I do not know,' said Hamish patiently. 'I was just beginning to find out when you arrived. I have talked with John Cartwright and you interrupted me when I was in the process of talking to Mrs Heather Cartwright.'

'Before I start with the rest, I'd better fix up accommodation for[1] me and my men. I'll stay here myself, but it's a bit pricey[2] for the lot of us[3]. We've got five officers combing the bushes along with the forensic team at the moment. I saw that police station of yours[4]. You do yourself very well[5]. Any chance of a spare[6] bed or two?'

'I have not the room. I have the one bed[7] for myself and the other bedroom has not the bed but the gardening stuff[8] and the poultry feed and the bags of fertilizer[9] ...'

'Okay, okay, spare me the rural details.' Blair looked piercingly at Hamish, who gave him a sweet smile.

Simple[10], thought Blair. Would have to be to live here all year round[11].

He placed his beefy hands[12] on the desk and looked at Hamish in a kindly way. 'I'm thinking you're a wee bit[13] too inexperienced for this sort of high-class crime,' he said. 'We'll use your office at the station[14] because I'm damned if I'll pay hotel phone prices. I have to fight hard enough to get my expenses as it is[15]. Just you attend to[16] your usual rounds[17] and leave the detective[18] work to us. We're all experienced men.'

Hamish looked at the detective chief inspector blankly[19]. Only a few minutes before he had been wondering how to keep out of the case. He had taken a dislike to the chief detective and his

1. ferais mieux de trouver où loger
2. cher
3. nous tous
4. votre commissariat
5. êtes bien loti
6. d'appoint
7. juste un lit
8. affaires de jardinage
9. engrais
10. Simplet
11. Forcément, pour habiter ici toute l'année...
12. grosses paluches
13. un tantinet
14. commissariat
15. déjà assez de mal comme ça pour me faire défrayer
16. Contentez-vous de faire
17. rondes
18. d'enquêteur
19. l'air absent

sidekicks[1] and did not want to tag around after them[2]. But now he had been told to keep clear[3], well, all that did was give him a burning desire to find out who had killed Lady Jane.

'I'll be off then,' said Hamish. Blair watched him go and shook his head sadly. 'Poor fellow,' he said. 'Never had to do any real work in his life before, and, like all these Highlanders, fights shy of it as much as possible[4]. Send in that American couple, MacNab. Typical pair of tourists. May as well get rid of them first.'

Hamish ambled along the front, gazing dreamily out over the loch. The early evening sun was flooding the bay with gold. A pair of seals were rolling and turning lazily, sending golden ripples washing about the white hulls[5] of the yachts and the green and black hulls of the fishing boats.

He saw the slim, elegant figure of Priscilla Halburton-Smythe walking towards him, and, suddenly overcome with a mixture of shyness[6] and longing[7], he stopped and leaned his elbows on the mossy[8] stone wall above the beach.

She stopped and stood beside him. 'What's all this I hear?' said Priscilla. 'The hillside's crawling with[9] bobbies[10], putting things in plastic bags.'

'Lady Jane Winters has been murdered.'

'I heard something to that effect[11]. Big, fat, nasty woman, wasn't she?'

'Aye, you could say that.'

'And who did it, Holmes?'

'I chust don't know, and I've been more or less told to go home and feed my chickens by the detectives from Strathbane.'

1. sbires
2. leur coller aux basques
3. qu'on lui disait de ne pas s'en mêler
4. fait tout pour l'éviter
5. coques
6. timidité
7. de désir
8. couvert de mousse
9. grouille de
10. flics
11. de ce genre

'Well, you must be pleased about that. I mean, you never were exactly one of the world's greatest workers.'

'How would you know that, Miss Halburton-Smythe? It is not as if I have the murder on my hands every day of the week.'

'You must admit when Daddy wants to talk to you about poaching or something, you're never where you should be. I told Daddy not to worry you[1] about poachers since you're one yourself.'

'That is not a very nice thing to say.'

'I was only joking. Do you really want to find the murderer? Do you need a Watson? I shall follow you about[2] saying, "By Jove, you're a wonder[3]. How on earth did you think of that?" '

'Oh, I suppose I'll do as I'm told and keep out of the way,' said Hamish equably[4].

'Funny, I thought you'd have been dying to find out for yourself. All that Highland curiosity.' Priscilla sounded disappointed.

'Aye, well ...' began Hamish, and then his gaze suddenly sharpened. Mrs Baxter and Charlie could be seen leaving the hotel.

'Are you going to ask them questions?' asked Priscilla, following his gaze. 'Can I listen?'

'Och, no. The wee lad[5] has a very interesting stamp and I wanted to have another look at it.'

'Hamish Macbeth, I give you up[6]!'

He gave her a crooked grin[7]. 'I did not know you had ever taken me on[8], Miss Halburton-Smythe.'

He pushed his hat up on his forehead, thrust his hands in his pockets, and strolled off[9] to meet the Baxters.

Highly irritated, Priscilla watched him go.

1. de ne pas vous embêter
2. partout,
3. incroyable
4. d'un ton placide
5. p'tit gars
6. je renonce à vous
7. sourire en coin
8. que vous m'aviez adopté
9. partit d'un pas tranquille

Day Five

A counsel of perfection is very easy advice to give, but is usually quite impracticable[1].
– Maxwell Knight[2], *Bird Gardening*

Alice started to dress hurriedly, although it was only seven in the morning. She wanted to escape from the hotel before they were besieged by the press again[3]. They had started to filter in gradually[4] , and by late evening they had grown to an army: an army of questioning faces. Alice's juvenile crime loomed large in her mind[5]. If Lady Jane could have found out about *that*, then they could too. Normally Alice would have been thrilled to bits[6] at the idea of getting her photograph in the papers. But her murky[7] past tortured her. Jeremy had been particularly warm and friendly to her the evening before. She felt sure he would not even look at her again if he found out. The major had howled at[8] the hotel manager over the problem of the press, and the manager had at last reluctantly banned them[9]. He was thoroughly fed up with[10] the notoriety[11] the murder had brought to his hotel and had hoped to ease the pain[12] with the large amount of money the gentlemen of the press were spending in the bar. But guests other than the major had complained, guests who came every year. And so the reporters and the photographers were now billeted out[13] in the village,

1. impossible à mettre en œuvre

2. [naturaliste et agent secret britannique, mort en 1968]

3. qu'ils ne soient de nouveau harcelés par les journalistes

4. entrer au compte-gouttes

5. l'obsédait

6. ravie

7. trouble

8. crié sur

9. leur avait enfin, à contre-cœur, interdit l'accès

10. en avait plus qu'assez de

11. la mauvaise réputation que

12. se consoler

13. logés ailleurs

most of them at a boarding house[1] at the other end of the bay.

Alice was just on the point of leaving the room when the telephone began to ring. She stared at it and then suddenly rushed and picked it up. Her mother's voice, sharp with agitation, sounded over the line. 'What's all this, luv[2]? Your name's in the morning papers. You didn't even tell us you was going to such a place. We're that[3] worried.'

'It's all right, Mum,' said Alice. 'It's got nothing to do with me.'

'I know that, luv, but that woman that was murdered, her photo's in the papers and she was around here last week, asking questions. Said she was writing a piece[4] on young girls who had made the move to London and their reasons for doing it.'

She must have got all our addresses from Heather, thought Alice with a sudden sickening lurch of the heart[5]. Heather even sent me the names of the other guests, sort of to make it sound social[6].

Her voice shrill with anxiety, Alice asked, 'Did she find out anything about me being in court[7]?'

'You was never in court, luv.'

'Yes. 'Member? It was when I broke Mr Jenkins' window and he took me to the juvenile court.'

'Oh, *that*. She didn't ask me and I don't suppose anyone around here remembers a silly little thing like that. She talked to Maggie Harrison, mind[8].'

Alice held tightly on to the phone. Maggie Harrison had been her rival for years. If Maggie could have remembered anything nasty[9] about her, Alice, then Maggie would have undoubtedly told everything.

1. pension
2. [love]
3. si
4. article
5. un coup au cœur
6. histoire de rendre ça plus convivial
7. mon passage au tribunal
8. remarque
9. de moche

'Are you there?' Her mother's voice sounded like a squawk[1]. 'I'm in a call box[2] and the money's running out[3]. Can you call me back?'

'No, Mum, I've got to go. I'll be all right.'

'Take care of yourself, will you? I don't like you getting mixed up with those sort of people.'

The line went dead[4].

Alice slowly replaced the receiver and wiped her damp palm[5] on her sweater. Well, Lady Jane couldn't write anything now.

She turned quickly and ran from the room. Outside the hotel a thin, greasy drizzle[6] was falling.

She looked quickly along the waterfront, dreading to see a reporter waiting to pounce[7] on her, but everything was deserted as far as she could see. She hesitated. Perhaps it would have been better to stay in the hotel. It was now banned to the press, so why bother to venture out[8]? But the fear of anyone – Jeremy in particular – finding out about her past drove her on[9].

There was a pleasant smell of woodsmoke, tar[10], kippers[11], bacon and strong tea drifting from the cottages. Alice approached Constable Macbeth's house and saw him standing in his garden, feeding the chickens. He turned at the sound of her footsteps, and she smiled weakly.

'Is your third degree over[12]?' asked the policeman.

'It wasn't so bad,' said Alice. 'I really didn't know that awful woman was a newspaper columnist, and I think they believed me.'

'I was just about to make a cup of tea. Would you like one?'

'Yes,' said Alice gratefully, thinking how very unlike a policeman Constable Macbeth looked[13]. He was hatless and wearing an old army sweater

1. cri d'orfraie
2. cabine
3. je n'ai presque plus de sous
4. Elle avait raccroché
5. essuya sa paume moite
6. crachin
7. fondre
8. mettre le nez dehors
9. la fit persister
10. de goudron
11. de harengs fumés
12. Ils ont fini de vous cuisiner
13. que l'agent Macbeth n'avait pas du tout l'air d'un policier

1. délavé
2. avait bien fait comprendre
3. avait dû l'irriter
4. aigrement
5. désordonné
6. mais plutôt propre
7. de la vaisselle
8. outils
9. pots de confiture
10. J'entasse
11. le garde
12. un mal terrible à
13. versa coup sur coup
14. avec intensité
15. s'est donné du mal

and a faded[1] pair of jeans. That chief detective had made it plain[2] that the village constable would not be having anything to do with the investigation. Mr Macbeth must have riled him[3] in some way because he had been quite unpleasant about it, Alice remembered. Blair had asked her if she had noticed or heard anything unusual that might point to the murderer, and Alice had shaken her head, but had said if she did remember anything she would tell Constable Macbeth, and that was when Blair had sourly[4] pointed out that the village policeman was not part of the murder investigation.

Alice followed Hamish into his kitchen, which was long and narrow with a table against the window.

She looked around the kitchen curiously. It was messy[5] in a clean sort of way[6]. There were piles of magazines, china[7], bits of old farm implements[8], Victorian dolls, and stacks of jam jars[9].

'I'm a hoarder[10],' said Mr Macbeth. 'I aye think a thing'll fetch a good price if I just hang on to it[11]. I have a terrible time[12] throwing things away. Milk and sugar?'

'Yes, please,' said Alice. He gave her a cup, sat down next to her at the table, and heaped[13] five spoonfuls of sugar into his own tea.

'Do I look like a murderer?' asked Alice intently[14].

'I think a murderer could look like anyone,' said the policeman placidly. 'Now this Lady Jane, it strikes me she went to a lot of work[15] to find out about the people who were going to be at the fishing school. How did she know who was going?'

'Oh, that's easy. Heather sent us all a list of names and addresses. The idea is that we can get in touch with anyone in our area and maybe travel up with them. That's how Jeremy came to travel up with Daphne. He didn't know her before.' Alice blushed furiously and buried her nose in her cup.

'Yes, and she must have found out about me and my family after she came,' said Hamish. 'She had only to ask a few people in the village. You can't keep anything secret in the Highlands.'

'I wish she had never come,' said Alice passionately. 'She's ruined my life.'

'Indeed! And how is that[1]?'

The rain was falling more steadily and the cluttered[2] kitchen was peaceful and warm. Alice had a longing to unburden herself[3].

'If a young man was interested in a girl,' she said, not looking at him, 'would you think that young man might go off[4] that girl if he found out she had done something ... well, against the law, when she was a kid?'

'It depends on the young man. Now if you're talking about Mr Jeremy Blythe ...'

'You *noticed*. He *is* rather sweet on me[5].' Alice removed her hat and tossed back her fluffy hair in what she fondly[6] thought was a *femme-fataleish* sort of way[7].

'It depends on the crime,' said Hamish. 'Now if you'd poisoned your mother or ...'

'No, nothing like that,' said Alice. 'Look, when I was about Charlie's age, I threw a brick through Mr Jenkins' window for a dare[8]. Mr Jenkins was a nasty old man who lived in our street. The other girls egged me on[9]. Well, he got me charged[10] and taken to court. All I got was a warning[11] and Mum had to pay for the window and the local paper put a couple of lines about it at the bottom of one of their pages. I mean, it was a silly little thing, really,

1. Comment ça
2. encombrée
3. envie de se confier
4. ne plus aimer
5. a vraiment un faible pour moi
6. plaisamment
7. un style assez « femme fatale »
8. par défi
9. m'ont poussée à le faire
10. a porté plainte contre moi
11. avertissement

but would a man like Jeremy mind? You see, he's awfully ambitious and … and … well, he plans to stand for Parliament[1], and … and … oh, do you know now I've told you, I realize I've been worrying about nothing. I should have told *him*. In fact, I'd better before anyone else does. How he'll laugh!'

'If it's that unimportant,' said Hamish, pouring himself more tea, 'then I am thinking that there is no need whateffer[2] to tell anyone at all. In my opinion, Miss Wilson, Mr Blythe is something of a[3] snob and would not normally be interested in you were he not[4] on holiday …'

Alice leapt to her feet[5]. '*You're* the snob,' she said. 'And rude[6], too. I'll show you. I'll tell Jeremy right now and when I'm[7] Mrs Blythe, you can eat your words[8].'

'As you please.' Hamish shrugged. Alice rushed out of the house and slammed[9] the kitchen door with a bang. Hamish cursed himself for being clumsy[10]. Alice reminded him of Ann Grant, a young girl brought up in Lochdubh, only passably pretty. She had been seen around one of the flashier[11] holiday guests two summers ago, driving with him everywhere in his car, and gossiping about the grand[12] wedding she would have. But the holidaymaker[13] had left and Ann had gone about ill and red-eyed. She had been packed off[14] suddenly to a relative in Glasgow. The village gossips said she had gone to have an abortion[15] and was now walking the streets[16]. But Hamish had heard through *his* relatives that she was working as a typist in a Glasgow office and had said she never wanted to see Lochdubh or her family again. If her family hadn't been so common, she said, then her beau[17] would have married her.

1. d'être candidat aux législatives
2. [whatever]
3. un peu
4. s'il n'était pas
5. se leva d'un bond
6. grossier
7. serai
8. ravalerez vos paroles
9. claqua
10. se maudit pour sa maladresse
11. clinquants
12. en grande pompe
13. vacancier
14. envoyée
15. avorter
16. aujourd'hui faisait le trottoir
17. soupirant

Snobbery is a terrible thing, thought Hamish dismally[1]. It can almost kill young girls. Would they kill because of it? That was a question well worth turning over[2].

Alice ran all the way back to the hotel and straight up to Jeremy's room. She pounded[3] on the door until a muffled[4] voice shouted, 'The door's open. I'm in the bathroom.'

She pushed open the door. Perhaps the murder had made her a little crazy or perhaps Alice had lived in a fantasy[5] world for too long, but she justified her next action by persuading herself that they were going to be married, or would be married if she established a basis of intimacy. She strolled casually[6] into the bathroom and sat on the edge of the bath.

'Hello, darling,' she said.

Jeremy hastily floated a large sponge over himself to act as a fig leaf[7] and asked carefully, without looking at her, 'Have you been drinking? I know we're all shattered[8] by this murder business but ...'

Alice came down to reality with a bump[9]. 'I'll wait for you in the bedroom,' she gasped. 'I've got something I *must* tell you.'

She sat nervously on the bed by the window, fidgeting with[10] the curtain cord and wishing she hadn't been so *bold*[11].

Jeremy came out with a white towel knotted around his waist and drying his hair with another.

Alice turned her face away and twisted a handkerchief nervously in her hands.

'*Now* you look like your usual self,' said Jeremy. 'For a moment there I thought you were going to rape me[12].'

1. avec consternation
2. qui méritait d'être posée
3. tambourina
4. étouffée
5. imaginaire
6. entra tranquillement
7. en guise de feuille de vigne
8. dévastés
9. retrouva brusquement ses esprits
10. à tripoter
11. regrettant d'avoir montré autant d'audace
12. me violer

1. s'avérait avoir raison
2. risquait de se savoir
3. sans s'arrêter
4. goudron qui fondait
5. de honte
6. d'un air gêné
7. chemisette d'écolière
8. tendue sur
9. vécu l'enfer
10. calmant
11. du talc

'Don't make fun of me,' said Alice, wishing he wouldn't look so amused, so *detached*. What if Macbeth should prove to be right[1]?

But if they were married, it might come out[2]. Better tell him now. And so Alice did, simply plunging into her story at the beginning and charging on[3] until the end.

As she talked, she was back there in that dusty court on that hot summer's day with the tar melting[4] on the roads outside. She could still remember her mother, crying with shame[5]. She could remember her own sick feeling of disgrace.

When she finished, she looked at Jeremy awkwardly[6]. He was studying her face in an intent, serious way. Jeremy was actually wondering whether to share his own guilty secret and at the same time noticing how Alice's schoolgirlish blouse[7] was strained against[8] her small, high breasts. God, it had been ages since ... Then there was all this fear and worry about the murder. Yes, he knew why Alice had dreaded Lady Jane printing that bit of childhood nonsense. Hadn't he himself gone through hell[9] to try to shut her mouth? He glanced at the clock. Eight-thirty. Too early for a drink but not too early for that other tranquillizer[10].

He sat down beside Alice on the bed and drew her against his still-damp body. 'You don't mind?' whispered Alice.

'Of course not,' he said, stroking her hair. She smelled of nervous sweat, sharp and acrid, mixed with lavender talcum powder[11]. He put a hand on one little breast and began to stroke it.

Alice shivered against him. She was not a virgin, having lost that through curiosity and drink two years ago in the back of a car after a party with a man whose name she could not remember. It had been a painful and degrading experience, but he had been a heavy, vulgar sort of man.

Women's Lib[1] has a long way to go[2] before it gets *inside* girls like Alice. As his lips began to move against her own, her one[3] thought was, 'If I sleep with him, hc'll have to marry me.'

As they lay stretched out on the bed, pressed together, as Alice's clothes were removed, she had an idiotic wish that Jeremy might have been wearing some sort of status symbol, his gold wrist watch, say[4]. For[5] when the all-too-brief foreplay[6] was over and she was rammed[7] into the bed by the panting[8], struggling weight of this man, it all seemed as painful and degrading as that time in the back of the car. She wished he'd hurry up and get it over with[9]. There was that terrible tyranny of the orgasm. What *was* it? He was obviously waiting for something to happen to her. She had read about women shrieking in ecstasy[10], but if she shrieked, she might bring people rushing in, thinking there had been another murder.

His silence was punctuated by grunts[11], not words of love. At last, just when she thought she could not bear it any longer, he collapsed[12] on top of her. She let out a long sigh of relief, and Jeremy kissed her ear and said, 'It was good for you too,' mistaking her sigh for one of satisfaction.

'I love you, Jeremy,' whispered Alice, winding her arms around him and hugging that vision[13] of sports car, expensive clothes, good accent, and Member of Parliament.

'Do you?' He propped himself up on one elbow[14]. 'That's nice.' He kissed her nose and then smacked her on the bottom[15]. 'Better get dressed. Gosh, I'm hungry.'

1. Les féministes
2. encore du chemin à faire
3. seule
4. mettons
5. Car
6. préliminaires bien trop brefs
7. enfoncée
8. ahanant
9. qu'il en finisse
10. poussant des cris d'extase
11. des grognements
12. s'effondra
13. en enlaçant et lui et la perspective
14. se releva sur un coude
15. lui claqua les fesses

Alice scooped up[1] her clothes and scuttled[2] into the bathroom. After she had showered and dressed, she felt better. Love in the morning. How sophisticated. How deliciously decadent.

She was just putting on lipstick when Jeremy shouted through the door, 'I'll see you in the dining room. Don't be long.'

Alice's hand jerked nervously[3], and she smeared lipstick[4] over her cheek. She scrubbed it off with a tissue[5] and then ran out, hoping to catch him, but he had already left.

When she went out into the corridor, two maids[6] were stuffing[7] dirty sheets into a hamper[8] and they looked at her curiously. 'Good morning,' said Alice, staring at both of them hard as if challenging them[9] to voice[10] their evil thoughts.

The fishing party[11] was grouped around one large table in the far corner as if the management[12] had decided to put them in quarantine. The Roths were there and Daphne, the major and Jeremy. Charlie would be having breakfast[13] with his aunt, but where were the Cartwrights?

'Don't know,' shrugged Daphne. ' I think they jolly well ought to be[14] here handing out refunds[15]. Pass the marmalade, Jeremy darling.' Alice frowned. It was time to stake her claim[16]. She slid into a chair beside Jeremy and took his hand under the table, gave it a squeeze, and smiled at him in an intimate way. 'I need both hands to eat, Alice,' said Jeremy crossly. Alice snatched her hand away and Daphne giggled.

Heather and John Cartwright were sitting in Hamish's cluttered kitchen, eating bacon baps[17] and drinking tea. They had explained they were 'just passing'.

1. prit vite
2. se faufila
3. eut une saccade
4. se fit une marque de rouge à lèvres
5. mouchoir en papier
6. femmes de chambre
7. fourraient
8. corbeille à linge
9. comme pour les mettre au défi
10. de dire tout haut
11. groupe des pêcheurs
12. direction
13. devait être en train de petit-déjeuner
14. La moindre des choses serait qu'ils soient
15. à nous faire des rembourse-ments
16. de marquer son territoire
17. des pains ronds au bacon

It was Heather who had had the impulse to talk to Hamish. Hamish was a good sounding board[1] because he *was* the law[2], and although he could hardly be described as a strong arm of it[3], he was in a position to overhear how the investigation was proceeding[4].

'I just hope this won't break the fishing school,' said John gloomily.

'I should not think so,' said Hamish, turning bacon deftly[5] in the pan. 'Provided[6], of course, the murderer is found. It will be in the way of being[7] an added attraction.'

'I was shocked when Blair told me she was really that awful columnist woman.'

Hamish stood very still, his back to them as he worked at the stove. 'And you did not know this before?' he asked.

There was a little silence, and then John said, 'Of course not. Had we known then we should not have allowed her to come.'

'Aye, but did you not know after she had arrived?' asked Hamish.

Again that silence. Hamish turned round, the bacon slice in one hand.

'No, we did not,' said Heather emphatically[8]. Hamish carefully and slowly lifted the bacon from the pan and put it on a plate. He turned off the gas. He lifted his cup of tea from beside the stove and came and joined Heather and John at the table.

'I happen to know that you had a letter from Austria. You see, you threw it out of the window, hoping it would land in the loch. The tide was out[9] and the boy Charlie picked it up because the stamp attracted his attention. I would not normally read anyone else's mail, but when it comes to

1. constituait un bon test
2. la police
3. n'en était pas vraiment le bras armé
4. avançait
5. avec adresse
6. À condition [que]
7. sera plutôt
8. avec force
9. basse

murder, well, I don't have that many fine scruples[1]. It was from a couple of friends of yours in Austria who ran[2] a ski resort[3] until Lady Jane came on holiday.' 'You have no right to read private mail,' shouted John.

Hamish looked at him stolidly[4].

Heather put a hand on John's arm. 'It's no use[5],' she said wearily[6]. 'We did know. We were frightened. This school is our life. Years of hard work have gone into building it up. We thought she was going to take it away from us.'

'But the couple at the ski resort turned out to be married to other people, not each other,' pointed out Hamish. 'They said the publicity by Lady Jane ruined them only because Mr Bergen, the ski resort owner, had not been paying alimony[7] for years. You are surely both not in that sort of position. When you found out, would it not have been better to try to tell the school, openly and in front of her, what she did for a living?'

'I didn't think of that,' said John wretchedly[8]. 'You may as well know[9] that I saw Jane on the night she was murdered. I went up to her room after dinner.'

'And ...?'

'And she just laughed at me. She said this sort of fly fishing in these waters was like grouse shooting or deer stalking[10] – a sport for the rich. She said she was about to prove that the sort of people who went on these holidays were social climbers[11] who deserved[12] to be cut down to size[13].'

'Deary me,' said Hamish, stirring his tea, 'was she a Communist?'

'I don't think she was a member of the Communist Party, if that's what you mean,' said John. 'She seemed to want to make people writhe[14]. She was

1. autant de scrupules
2. dirigeaient
3. station de ski
4. impassiblement
5. Ce n'est plus la peine
6. d'un ton las
7. une pension alimentaire
8. avec tristesse
9. Autant que vous sachiez
10. chasser la grouse ou le cerf
11. des arrivistes
12. méritaient
13. qu'on les remette à leur place
14. appuyer là où ça fait mal

like a blackmailer[1] who enjoys power. In Scotland they would say she was just agin[2] everything.'

'Did she say she was out to[3] ruin the fishing school?'

'Not in so many words[4]. But that's what she was setting out[5] to do.'

'What exactly did you say?'

'I said that I had worked hard to build up this school and I begged her[6] not to harm it[7]. She laughed at me and told me to get out. I said ... I said ...'

'Yes?' prompted[8] Hamish gently.

'You'd better tell him,' said Heather.

'I told her I would kill her,' whispered John. 'I shouted it. I'll have to tell Blair – I think Jeremy heard me.'

'Mr Blythe? Why would he hear you? Is his room next to hers?'

'No, he was out in the corridor when I left.'

'What will we do, Mr Macbeth?' pleaded[9] Heather.

'I think you should tell Mr Blair. If there's one thing that makes a detective like Blair suspicious, or any detective for that matter[10], it's finding out someone's been hiding something. The pair of you have got nothing awful in your past that Lady Jane was about to expose[11]?'

Both shook their heads.

'And apart from the short time that Mr Cartwright was with Lady Jane, you were together all night?'

'Why do you ask?' Heather had turned white.

'I ask,' said Hamish patiently, 'because any copper with a nasty mind[12] might think that *one* of you might have sneaked off[13] and bumped her off[14], if not the pair of you.'

1. maître-chanteur
2. [against]
3. avait pour but de
4. explicitement
5. avait l'intention
6. l'ai suppliée
7. de ne pas lui nuire
8. le pressa
9. l'implora
10. d'ailleurs
11. s'apprêtait à révéler
12. à l'esprit mal tourné
13. s'éclipser
14. pour la buter

'We had better go,' said Heather. 'Tell Mr Blair we're taking the class up to the Marag to fish. It's near enough. We must go on as if nothing had happened.'

After they left, Hamish, who had already heard the sound of voices from his office at the front, ambled through[1] with a cup of tea in one hand.

'Shouldn't you be in uniform?' growled Blair, who was seated behind Hamish's desk flanked by his two detectives.

'In a minute,' said Hamish easily[2].

'And I told you to keep out of this[3]. That was the Cartwrights I saw leaving.'

'Aye[4].'

'Well, what did they have to say for themselves[5]?'

'Only that they knew something they hadn't told you and now thought they should. Also that they were taking the class up to the Marag which is quite close[6] so that you can go and see any of the members quite easily.'

'For Jesus buggering Christ's sake, don't they know this is a murder investigation?'

'Find any clues[7]?' asked Hamish.

'Just one thing. If it had been like today, we might have found more traces. But most of the ground was baked hard[8]. The procurator fiscal's report says she was strangled somewhere else and dragged along through the bushes and then thrown in the pool.'

'And what is this clue?'

'It's just a bit of a photograph,' said MacNab, before Blair could stop him. 'Just a bit torn off the top corner[9]. See.'

He held out the bit of black and white photograph on a pair of tweezers[10]. Hamish took it gingerly[11].

1. s'y rendit d'un pas tranquille
2. tranquillement
3. de rester en dehors de tout ça
4. Oui
5. leur défense
6. n'est pas loin
7. Vous avez trouvé des indices
8. complètement durci
9. un coin arraché en haut d'une photo
10. pince à épiler
11. précautionneusement

It showed the very top of a woman's head, or what he could only guess to be a woman's head because it had some sort of sparkly[1] ornament on top like the edge of a tiara[2]. Behind was a poster with the part legend BUY BRIT—.

'That might have been Buy British,' said Hamish, 'which means it would have been taken in the sixties when Wilson was running that Buy British campaign and that would therefore eliminate the younger members of the fish ...'

'Listen to the great detective,' jeered[3] Blair. 'We all reached that conclusion in two seconds flat[4]. Why don't you trot off and find out if anyone's been raiding the poor box[5] in one of those churches. Damn ridiculous having so many churches in a wee place like this[6].'

Hamish turned to amble out. 'And get your uniform on,' shouted Blair.

'Now,' said Blair, rustling through sheafs of statements[7]. 'According to these, they're all innocent. But one of them was so afraid that Lady Jane would print something about them that they killed her. So chase up all these people we phoned yesterday and hurry them up[8]. And that includes background on the Roths. See if there's been a telex from the FBI. Find out if any of them have been in trouble with the police, although I think you'll have to dig deeper[9] than that.'

Hamish changed into his uniform, admitting to his reflection[10] in the glass that he, Hamish Macbeth, was a very angry man. In fact, he could not quite remember being so angry in all his easygoing[11] life. He was determined to go on talking to the members of the fishing school until someone said something that gave himself away[12]. He was not going to be frightened because it was a

1. étincelant
2. bord d'un diadème
3. railla
4. à peine
5. tronc des pauvres
6. bled pareil
7. en feuilletant des liasses de dépositions
8. secouez-les
9. chercher plus loin
10. reflet
11. paisible
12. le trahisse

murder investigation. All criminals were the same whether it was a theft[1] in the school or poaching deer[2] on the hills. You talked, asked questions, and listened and watched and waited. The hell with Blair[3]. He would go up to the Marag and find out what Jeremy had been doing outside Lady Jane's room. As he left by the back door, the press were entering the police station by the front. At least Lochdubh would be spared[4] their headlines[5] until the following morning. The newspapers were always a day late.

In any common-or-garden murder[6], the press would not hang about[7] longer than a day or two. But this murderee[8] had a title and the location[9] was well away from their office with out-of-town expenses[10], so they would all try to spin it out[11] as long as they could. Of course, Lady Jane had been one of their own[12], so to speak[13], and Hamish had learned from his relative in Fleet Street some time ago that the press were not like the police: they were notoriously uninterested in anything that happened to one of their ranks except as a subject for gossip.

The day was warm and sweaty, and although the rain had stopped, there was a thick mist everywhere and the midges were out in clouds. Hamish took a stick of repellent[14] out of his tunic pocket and rubbed his face and neck with it.

When he reached the Marag, it was to find the fishing school diligently at work, looking like some old army-jungle movie, as each one had a mosquito net[15] shrouding[16] the face.

Hamish scanned the anonymous figures, picked out Heather and John by virtue of[17] their expert casting rather than their appearance, and Charlie because of his size and because his mother was

1. vol
2. du braconnage
3. Que Blair aille au diable
4. se verrait épargner
5. gros titres
6. banale affaire d'assassinat
7. les journalistes ne resteraient pas
8. victime-là
9. lieu du crime
10. ce qui faisait des frais de déplacement
11. de faire durer
12. était des leurs
13. pour ainsi dire
14. anti-moustique
15. moustiquaire
16. lui enveloppant
17. d'après

sitting on a rock nearby, flapping away the mosquitoes and watching her son as if expecting him to be dragged off to prison at any moment. Hamish went to join her.

'I think this is ridiculous,' she burst out as soon as she saw him. 'It's horrible weather and the whole school should be broken up and sent home.'

'They seem quite happy,' said Hamish.

'I don't understand it,' wailed[1] Mrs Baxter. 'Those Cartwrights suggested the school should try to go on as if nothing has happened, and they all leapt at it[2] when[3] just a moment before they had been threatening to ask for their money back. I told my Charlie *he* was coming straight home with me, and he *defied* me. Just like his father.' Two large tears of self-pity[4] formed in Mrs Baxter's eyes and she dabbed at them[5] furiously with a tissue. 'I knew I should never have let Charlie come all the way up here. The minute I got his letter, I was on the train.'

'Aye, and when did you arrive?'

'I *told* the police. I got to Lochdubh just after the terrible murder.'

'Then how is it[6] that Mrs MacPherson down at the bakery saw you the night before?'

'It wasn't me. It must have been someone else.'

'Blair will check the buses and so on, you know,' said Hamish. 'It's always better to tell the truth. If you don't, it looks as if you might have something to hide. Did you know Lady Jane was a newspaperwoman?'

Mrs Baxter sat in silence, twisting the damp tissue in her fingers. Rain dripped from her sou'wester[7]. 'She's been around the neighbourhood asking questions,' said Mrs Baxter at last in

1. gémit

2. ont sauté sur la proposition

3. alors que

4. apitoiement sur son sort

5. les tapota

6. comment se fait-il

7. suroît [chapeau imperméable]

a low voice. 'I've never got on[1] with my neighbours and I know they told her all about the divorce. But what's divorce? Half the population of Britain get divorced every year. I've nothing to be ashamed of and that I told her[2].'

'You *told* Lady Jane?'

'Well, I phoned her before I got on the train,' said Mrs Baxter miserably, 'and I said if she wrote anything about my Charlie I would ...'

'Kill her?'

'People say all sorts of things they don't mean when they're angry,' said Mrs Baxter defiantly. 'This is a wretched business[3]. Do you know that detective, MacNab, was round at the house last night asking for Charlie's leader?'

'No, I did not. I'm shocked.'

'So you should be. Suspecting a mere[4] child.'

'It is not that that shocks me but the fact that they did not immediately check all the leaders earlier in the day. Was anyone's leader missing?'

'*I* don't know. *You* should know. They fingerprinted[5] everyone as well.'

Out of the corner of his eye, Hamish saw a white police car moving slowly round the edge of the loch.

He moved quickly out of sight behind a stand[6] of trees and made his way[7] silently along a rabbit track[8] that led back down to the village. Jeremy would have to wait. Hamish went straight to the hotel and asked the manager, Mr Johnson, where the press had disappeared to[9], since[10] he would have expected them to be up at the loch, photographing the school.

'There's a big Jack the Ripper sort of murder[11] broken[12] in London,' said Mr Johnson, 'and that's sent most of them scampering back home[13].

1. ne me suis jamais entendue
2. c'est ce que je n'ai pas manqué de lui dire
3. sale affaire
4. simple
5. ont relevé les empreintes de
6. rangée
7. avança
8. sentier
9. où étaient passés les journalistes
10. puisqu'
11. gros meurtre à la Jack l'Éventreur
12. qui a éclaté
13. du coup la plupart y sont repartis vite fait

The nationals[1] anyway. This is small beer by comparison. Also, Blair got the water bailiffs to block the private road to the Marag. He hates the press. Going to solve the murder for us, Mr Macbeth?'

'Aye, maybe.' Hamish grinned. 'Any hope of a wee shufty[2] at Lady Jane's room?'

'Blair had it locked, of course. No one's to go in[3]. Police commandment.'

'I'm the police, so there'll be no harm in letting me in.'

'I suppose. Come along then. But I think you'd better try to leave things as they are[4]. I've a feeling that Blair doesn't like you.'

Hamish followed the manager upstairs and along the corridors of the hotel. 'They took a plan of all the hotel rooms,' said Mr Johnson over his shoulder. 'I don't know what they expect to learn from that because it's said she was strangled up on the hillside in the middle of the night, not far from where she was shoved[5] in the pool. They've found a bittie of a[6] photograph, and Blair got everybody down to the last chambermaid fingerprinted[7]. No fingerprints on the photo, of course, and none on those chains that were around her legs, as if there would be anything worthwhile[8] after that time of churning and bashing about[9] that pool. But Mr Blair likes to throw his weight around[10]. Here we are.'

He put the key in the lock and opened the door. Lady Jane had occupied a suite with a good view of the loch. 'I'll leave you to it,' said Mr Johnson cheerfully. 'I can't feel sad about this murder. It's turned out good for business. Every lunch and dinner is booked up solid[11] for the next few weeks. They're coming from as far as Aberdeen, but then these oil[12] people have more money than sense[13].'

1. Ceux de la presse nationale
2. petit coup d'œil
3. ne doit entrer
4. de ne toucher à rien
5. a été poussée
6. un petit bout de
7. a fait relever les empreintes de tous, jusqu'à celles de la moindre femme de chambre
8. comme s'il allait y avoir quoi que ce soit de valable
9. tout ce temps à se faire malmener en tous sens dans
10. se mettre en avant
11. affiche complet
12. dans le pétrole
13. ne savent plus quoi faire de leur argent

Left alone, Hamish stood in the middle of the bedroom and looked around. Surely it must have dawned on[1] Blair before anything else that Lady Jane would have brought notes of some kind. Yes, of course it had. Fingerprint dust[2] lay like grey snow on every surface. Well, they would hardly[3] come back for *more* fingerprints. Hamish began his search. The suite consisted of a small entrance hall with a side table and one chair, a tiny sitting room with a writing desk, television set and two easy chairs[4], and a bedroom with a bathroom leading off it[5].

There was a typewriter[6] open on the writing desk with a pile of hotel writing paper beside it. He diligently searched the top of the desk and drawers. There was not a single piece of paper with any writing on it whatsoever[7]. Perhaps Blair had taken away what there was. He turned his attention to the bedroom. He slid open drawers of frivolous underwear[8] – Lady Jane's taste in that direction[9] was rather startling[10] – and rummaged[11] underneath. Nothing. If she had had a handbag, then Blair must have taken it away. Two suitcases lay on a luggage rack[12] at the foot of the bed. Locked.

He took a large ring of keys out of his tunic pocket and got to work, listening all the while[13] in case Blair should choose[14] that moment to return for another search. At last the first case[15] sprang open. There was a lavender sachet, two detective stories[16], a box of heated rollers[17], and a hair dryer. No paper of any kind. The next suitcase was completely empty.

He looked under the bed, under the mattress, down the sides of the chairs, even in the toilet

1. Il était forcément venu à l'esprit de
2. La poudre à empreintes
3. n'allaient sans doute pas
4. fauteuils
5. attenante
6. machine à écrire
7. comportant la moindre écriture
8. sous-vêtements
9. domaine
10. déconcertant
11. fouilla
12. porte-bagages
13. tout en tendant l'oreille
14. choisirait
15. valise
16. romans policiers
17. bigoudis

tank[1] and the bathroom cupboard, but not one scrap of paper did he find.

The manager had left the keys in the door. Hamish carefully locked the room and deposited the keys in the manager's office.

He decided to go back to the Marag to see if the field was clear[2]. But as he was making his way out of the hotel, he heard voices from the interviewing room and noticed Alice sitting nervously in the lounge outside.

'He's got Jeremy in there,' said Alice. 'Will this never end? He's going to see me next and then call in the others one by one. I told Jeremy about that court thing and he didn't mind[3], so you were wrong.'

'Is that a fact[4]?' said Hamish, looking down at her curiously.

Alice jerked her head to one side to avoid the policeman's gaze. Jeremy had been off-hand[5] all day, to say the least[6].

Hamish left quickly, deciding to try to find out a bit about the background of the others. He had in his tunic a list of the names and addresses of the members of the school. Perhaps he should start by trying to find out something about the Roths. But he could not use the telephone at the police station because Blair had set up headquarters[7] there, and although he was busy interviewing Jeremy, no doubt[8] his team of officers would be in the office.

Hamish's car was parked outside his house. He decided to take a run up to[9] the Halburton-Smythes. The rain had stopped falling and a light breeze had sprung up. But everything was wet and sodden[10] and grey. Mist shrouded[11] the mountains, and wet, long-haired sheep scampered across the road[12]

1. chasse d'eau
2. libre
3. s'en fichait
4. Vraiment
5. distant
6. et le mot était faible
7. avait pris ses quartiers
8. à coup sûr
9. de faire un saut chez
10. détrempé
11. enveloppait
12. traversèrent la route en trottinant

in front of the car on their spindly[1] black legs like startled fur-coated schoolmarms[2].

He swung off the main road and up the narrower one which led through acres of grouse moor[3] to the Halburton-Smythes' home. Home was a mock[4] castle, built by a beer baron[5] in the nineteenth century when Queen Victoria made the Highlands fashionable. It had pinnacles[6], turrets[7] and battlements[8] and a multitude of small, cold, dark rooms.

Hamish pushed open the massive, brass-studded[9] front door and walked into the stone-flagged[10] gloom[11] of the hall. He made his way through to the estate office, expecting to find Mr Halburton-Smythe's secretary, Lucy Hanson, there, but the room was deserted and the bright red telephone sitting on the polished mahogany desk[12] seemed to beg[13] Hamish to reach out and use it.

He sat down beside the desk and after some thought phoned Rory Grant at the *Daily Recorder* in Fleet Street. Rory sounded exasperated when he came on the line. 'What's the use of having a bobby for a relative[14] if I can't get an exclusive on a nice juicy murder? I had my bags packed and was going to set out on the road north when the Libyans decided to put a bomb in Selfridges[15] and some[16] Jack the Ripper started cutting up brass nails[17] in Brixton[18], so I'm kept[19] here. No one cares about your bloody murder now, but you might have given me a buzz[20]. I called the police station several times, and some copper told me each time to piss off[21].'

'It would still be news[22] if I found the murderer, Rory,' cajoled Hamish. 'You know the people who are at the fishing school. The names have been in all the papers. See if you can find out a bit more

1. maigrelettes
2. des maîtresses d'école effrayées en fourrure
3. des hectares de chasse réservée [à la chasse à la grouse]
4. faux
5. magnat de la bière
6. des pinacles
7. des tourelles
8. des créneaux
9. cloutée
10. pavée
11. pénombre
12. bureau d'acajou vernis
13. supplier
14. un flic dans sa parentèle
15. [grand magasin londonien]
16. une espèce de
17. à déchiqueter des prostituées
18. [quartier de Londres]
19. retenu
20. aurais pu me passer un coup de fil
21. d'aller me faire voir
22. aux infos

about them than has appeared. Oh, and while I'm on the phone, if I wanted to find out about someone from New York who might have been in trouble, or someone from Augusta, Georgia, what would I do?'

'You phone the FBI, don't you, you great Highland berk[1].'

'I think Detective Chief Inspector Blair will have done that and I would not want to go treading on any toes[2].'

'You can phone the newspapers, then, but you'll need to wait until I go and get names from the foreign desk. You are a pest[3], Hamish.'

Hamish held the line patiently until Rory returned with the information.

He thanked the reporter and, after listening to the silence of the castle for a few moments, dialled[4] New York. He was in luck. The reporter Rory had recommended said cheerfully it was a slack[5] day and did Hamish want him to call back. 'No, I will chust wait,' said Hamish, comfortably aware that he was not paying for the call.

After some time the reporter came back with the information on Marvin Roth. 'All old history,' he said cheerfully. 'Seems that back around 1970, he was in trouble over running sweatshops[6] in the garment district[7]. Employing illegal aliens[8] and paying them peanuts. Big stink[9]. Never got to trial. Bribed his way out of it[10]. Wants to go into politics[11]. Big man[12] in town now. Donates to charities, fashionable pinko[13], ban the bomb[14] and clean up the environment[15]. No one's going to rake up[16] his past. Got a nasty way of hitting back[17]. Knows all the big names and he's a buddy[18] of my editor's, so don't say where you got the information from, for Chrissake[19].'

1. crétin des Highlands
2. marcher sur ses plates-bandes
3. fléau
4. composa l'indicatif de
5. calme
6. pour avoir exploité la main-d'œuvre
7. dans le textile
8. des étrangers sans papiers
9. scandale
10. Il s'est évité le procès en payant des pots-de-vin
11. entrer en politique
12. Gros bonnet
13. gaucho branché
14. contre la bombe A
15. écolo
16. fouiller
17. sale tendance à se venger
18. pote
19. au nom du ciel

'Do you mean to tell me that you cannot print the facts?'

'Absolutely.'

'It is all very strange,' said Hamish, shaking his head. 'I have never been to New York. What is the weather like at the moment?'

They chatted amiably for five more minutes at Mr Halburton-Smythe's expense[1] before Hamish remembered the BUY BRIT— on the section of photograph. It seemed that it must be Buy British, but could it perhaps be an American advertisement[2]?

'Never heard of anything like it,' said the American reporter cheerfully, 'but I'll ask around.' Hamish gave him the Halburton-Smythes' phone number and told the reporter to give any information to Priscilla.

Then he phoned Augusta, Georgia. Here he was unlucky. The reporter sounded cross and harried[3]. No, he didn't know anything about Amy Roth, née Blanchard, off the top of his head[4]. Yes, he would phone back, but he couldn't promise.

Hamish put down the telephone and sighed. He heard the sound of heavy footsteps in the corridor and jumped to his feet. Colonel Halburton-Smythe erupted into the room. He was a small, thin, choleric[5] man in his late fifties. Hamish marvelled anew[6] that the fair Priscilla could have such an awful father.

'What are you doing here, Officer?' barked[7] the colonel, looking suspiciously at the phone. 'I was waiting for your good self[8],' said Hamish. 'Miss Halburton-Smythe told me you were still having trouble with the poachers.'

'I've just been down to your wretched station[9]. Fat chappie[10] told me he was in the middle of a

1. aux frais de Mr Halburton-Smythe
2. publicité
3. stressé
4. comme ça, de tête
5. sanguin
6. s'étonna à nouveau
7. aboya
8. vous
9. fichu commissariat
10. Un gros type

murder investigation. Told him one of my deer had been shot in the leg last night. Gave me a wall-eyed stare[1]. Useless, the lot of you. What are you going to do about it?'

'I will look into the matter[2],' said Hamish soothingly[3].

'See that you do[4], and while we're on the subject of poaching, I believe you've been squiring[5] my daughter to the local flea pit[6]. It's got to stop.'

'It was not a den of vice[7],' said Hamish patiently. 'And I would say Miss Halburton-Smythe is old enough to know her own mind[8].'

'If I find you sniffing around[9] my daughter again,' said the colonel rudely, 'I'll report you to your superiors.'

'You should not let yourself be getting in the bad temper[10],' said Hamish soothingly. 'Why,[11] I can see the wee[12] red veins breaking out all over your eyeballs. A terrible thing is the high blood pressure[13]. Why, I mind[14] ...'

'Get out!'

'Very well.' Hamish sauntered off[15] with maddening slowness[16].

Once out in the drive[17], however, he could not resist loitering[18] and looking around for a glimpse of Priscilla.

'If you think you're going to see my daughter,' barked the colonel behind him, 'have another think[19]. She's gone out for the day with John Harrington, Lord Harrington's son, and for your further information, she is shortly going to become engaged to him[20].'

Hamish realized with some amazement that hearts actually did ache[21]. Without replying, he walked to his car, climbed in and, without once looking at the colonel again, he drove off. When he

1. Il m'a fixé les yeux écarquillés
2. vais m'en occuper
3. d'un ton apaisant
4. N'y manquez pas
5. emmené
6. cinéma miteux du coin
7. antre du vice
8. pour savoir ce qu'elle veut
9. je vous reprends à tourner autour de
10. vous emporter ainsi
11. Allons,
12. petites
13. hypertension
14. C'est vrai, je me rappelle
15. s'éloigna d'un pas nonchalant
16. d'une lenteur exaspérante
17. allée
18. s'empêcher de s'attarder
19. vous vous faites des illusions
20. se fiancer avec lui
21. un cœur pouvait vraiment se briser

arrived at the police station, it was to find Blair and MacNab were still at the hotel and the suspicious-eyed detective, Jimmy Anderson, was sitting behind the desk in the office.

Hamish noticed a woman's handbag on the desk. 'Would that be Lady Jane's?' he asked.

'Yes,' grunted the detective without looking up.

'And would she maybe have a diary or anything with notes?'

'No, she did not,' said Jimmy Anderson. 'Deil a piece o' paper[1] or a note. Her money's there and her credit cards and cheque-book.'

'And it was in her room?'

'Aye, and Mr Blair still thinks someone killed her to stop her publishing something.'

'What have you got on them, just by way of a wee gossip[2]?' Hamish reached a hand into a vase and produced a bottle of Scotch. 'You'll be having a dram[3], of course.'

'That's very kind of you,' said Anderson, visibly thawing[4]. 'Don't see any harm in telling you, only don't tell Blair. Cheers.[5] Right, now. We're waiting to hear about the Roths. Blair's keen on them[6] all of a sudden despite that Buy British thing. He thinks there's a chance Roth might have Mafia connections and Lady Jane might have been on to it[7]. Would damage his career.'

'Would it now[8],' said Hamish, pouring himself a whisky. 'Mind you, it doesn't seem to have got in the way of[9] an American politician's career before. What about Amy Roth?'

'We're trying to find a bit on her too.'

'But Lady Jane would not have had the time to find out about the Roths. I mean, if it's that[10] difficult.'

1. Même pas un foutu bout de papier [écossais]

2. comme ça pour papoter

3. accepterez bien un petit verre

4. se détendant

5. Santé !

6. s'intéresse beaucoup à eux

7. l'avait peut-être découvert

8. Tiens donc

9. n'a pas l'air d'avoir jamais empêché

10. si

'All these bookings[1] were made at least eight months ago and that's when Lady Jane got the list. She's been in the States since then.'

'She certainly worked hard for her living,' said Hamish. 'A little more to warm you[2], Mr Anderson?'

'Thank you. Call me Jimmy. As to the rest, Jeremy Blythe's got an interest in politics as well. He was supposed to be sent down[3] from Oxford for having an affair[4] with the wife of one of the dons[5], but there's more to it than that. While he was having an affair with her, he also found time to get one of the local barmaids pregnant[6], and her husband raised a stink[7] at the college[8]. That way the don's wife found out and made a stink. Then he owed[9] money all over the place[10] although Daddy's rich. Wasn't studying. Sent down and finished his degree at London University. Became respectable but is still paying for the upkeep[11] of the barmaid's kid. Her husband settled for that out of court[12]. Daddy bought him a partnership[13], but he's been making rumblings[14] of becoming the next Conservative candidate. At a party last year, old friend from Oxford started ribbing him[15] about the barmaid and this Jeremy punched him rotten[16]. Police called in but no charges[17]. Filthy temper[18], he has.

'Alice Wilson chucked a brick through a neighbour's window when she was a kid and ended up in court. Not much there.

'Daphne Gore comes from a rich family. Caused a scandal by running off with a Spanish waiter[19] who, it turned out, had no intention of marrying her but had to be bought off[20] by Daphne's parents. Girl went into a depression and was in a psychiatric clinic for a few months. Could be a bit of insanity still around[21].

1. réservations
2. vous réchauffer
3. renvoyé
4. liaison
5. professeurs
6. mettre enceinte une de leurs serveuses
7. a fait un scandale
8. fac
9. devait
10. à droite et à gauche
11. éducation
12. Selon un arrangement à l'amiable avec le mari
13. part dans une société
14. laisse entendre son intention
15. à le charrier
16. lui a refait le portrait
17. pas de poursuites
18. Un sale caractère
19. serveur
20. soudoyé
21. des restes de démence

'Heather and John Cartwright. Very suspicious[1]. Owned up[2] they knew Lady Jane was out to get[3] the school and they're both fishing mad[4]. Not a sport with *them*, more a religion.

'Charlie Baxter. You can never tell with kids of that age, but I'm sure he's out of it[5]. The mother, on the other hand, is an hysterical type.'

'And the major?' prompted Hamish. 'He was more humiliated by Lady Jane than any of them.'

'Oh, the fishing and all that. We heard about how he'd threatened to kill her. Don't think there's anything to worry about there. Fine old soldier. Blair likes him. But we're waiting for a full report.'

There was the crunch[6] of wheels on the gravel outside. One minute Hamish was lounging in the chair opposite Anderson. The next he was gone – and[7] the bottle of whisky.

Hamish ambled along the front. A pale sun was beginning to turn the mist to gold, and there was a long patch of greenish-blue sky out on the horizon where the tiny white dot of a yacht bucketed about[8] to show the approaching wind beyond the shelter[9] of the harbour. The tide was out, leaving an expanse[10] of oily pebbled beach[11] scattered with the debris of storms and flotsam and jetsam from[12] boats.

He tried to focus his whole mind on the problem of the murder to banish the haunting picture of Priscilla languishing away[13] the afternoon in this man Harrington's arms.

Then he saw the Roths approaching. They were an odd pair[14], he thought. Amy was a big, soft woman, but Marvin's six feet[15] topped her by a few inches[16]. Although her movements were usually slow and calm, there seemed an underlying restlessness[17] about her. She was wearing

1. louches
2. Ils ont reconnu
3. voulait la mort de
4. dingues de pêche
5. qu'il n'a rien à voir avec ça
6. crissement
7. ainsi que
8. tanguait
9. abri
10. étendue
11. plage de galets huileux
12. les débris flottants laissés par les tempêtes et les
13. passant langoureusement
14. couple
15. le 1,82 m
16. la dominait de quelques centimètres
17. agitation sous-jacente

a trouser suit of faded denim[1] with a scarf knotted[2] about her throat. Marvin had changed into his usual sombre black business suit, and his bald head shone in the yellow light from the sea.

'When is all this going to end?' demanded Marvin as the couple came abreast[3] of Hamish. 'Amy isn't used to being treated the way she's been by your coppers. That Blair thinks he's hot shit[4].'

'I'm used to being treated like a lady,' said Amy. 'I thought all you Britishers were supposed to be gentlemen.'

'We're just like other folk,' said Hamish soothingly. 'Like sweeties[5]. We come in all shapes and sizes[6] and some of us are horrible.'

'Sweeties?' queried Amy, momentarily diverted.

'Candy,' translated[7] Marvin. 'See here, Amy's like aristocracy back home. This Blair wouldn't treat your Queen like this.'

'It's to my way of thinking[8] that he might,' said Hamish.

'Well, it's a pity Amy's folks have all passed away[9] or they would have something to say about this.'

Hamish looked at Amy as Marvin spoke and noticed the tightening of the skin at the corners of her eyelids and the way she was obviously ferreting around in her mind[10] for a change of subject. He had a sudden intuition that Amy had been lying[11] about her background. Well, a lot of people did, but they didn't go around committing murder when they were found out[12]. Or did they?

'Why doesn't Blair just arrest that major? He's the only one who had it in for[13] Lady Jane,' said Amy. 'You heard about his trick with the salmon?'

1. jean
2. nouée
3. à la hauteur
4. ne se prend pas pour de la merde
5. les bonbons
6. On existe dans toutes les formes et toutes les tailles
7. traduisit [en américain]
8. J'ai tendance à penser
9. soient tous morts
10. qu'elle se creusait visiblement la cervelle
11. avait menti
12. se faisaient démasquer
13. avait une dent contre

'Oh, aye, the gossip went two times around the village and back again[1]. It is very hard to keep anything quiet[2] in the Highlands.'

Amy muttered something like, 'Just like red hook,' and Hamish wondered whether it was something to do[3] with fishing.

'Except murder,' said Marvin. 'This place is the asshole[4] of the world. I don't like the country, I don't like the hick[5] servants at the hotel. What's a FEB?'

'Nothing that would apply to you[6], Mr Roth. It is just an expression the barman uses.'

'Him!' said Marvin with great contempt[7]. 'He can't even make a dry martini. One part gin to three parts[8] warm French[9] is his idea. Jeez[10], the fuckers[11] in this dump[12] piss me off[13].'

'Honey,' pleaded Amy, 'watch your language[14].'

Hamish's red eyebrows had vanished up under his cap with shock.

'Sorry,' said Marvin wearily. 'I guess I'm frightened. I feel trapped here. If we're going for this goddam constitutional[15], then we'd better get on with it[16].'

'Catch any fish?' asked Hamish.

'Jeremy and Heather caught a trout each,' said Marvin, 'but those salmon just can't be caught, in my opinion. They just jump about the place and keep well away from the hooks[17].'

'I could lend you one of my flies,' volunteered Hamish. 'I have had a bit of luck with it.'

'Say, why don't you join us for dinner tonight and bring it with you,' said Marvin. 'Everyone knows you're not on the case and we're getting a bit sick of each other[18]. After all, one of us did it[19] and we all sit around wondering who's going to be next.'

1. au moins
2. de taire quoi que ce soit
3. en rapport
4. trou du cul
5. ploucs
6. qui puisse s'appliquer à vous
7. mépris
8. et trois quarts
9. de vermouth
10. La vache
11. connards
12. trou à rats
13. me foutent en boule
14. Pas de gros mots
15. foutu petit tour
16. on ferait mieux d'y aller, là
17. évitent les hameçons
18. on en a un peu marre les uns des autres
19. est le coupable

Hamish accepted the invitation and went on his way.

As he approached the hotel, he saw Jeremy coming down towards it from the direction of the Marag, still wearing his fishing gear.

'Got one!' he shouted as Hamish approached. He held up a fair-sized trout.

'Let's get into the hotel,' said Hamish, noticing a reporter and photographer heading in their direction.

They walked together into the little room where Jeremy placed his catch[1] on the scales[2] and logged[3] the weight in the book. 'I was hearing that you were seen in the corridor outside Lady Jane's room the night she was murdered,' said Hamish.

'Nonsense,' said Jeremy, carefully lifting his fish off the scales. 'Aren't you supposed to be out of this investigation? I don't think Blair would like to hear you had been asking questions.'

'Maybe not. But he would like to hear what you'd been up to[4],' said Hamish.

'Then tell him and much good it may do you[5],' yelled Jeremy. He rushed off, nearly bumping into Alice, who was watching them anxiously. Alice ran after Jeremy and, undeterred[6] by the fact that he had slammed his room door in her face, she opened it and went in. He was sitting hunched[7] on the edge of the bed. 'That blasted, nosy copper[8],' he said without looking up.

Alice sat down beside him and took his hand in hers. 'What's the matter, Jeremy?' she pleaded. 'You've been awful to me all day.'

'Christ, I've got enough on my mind without worrying about you,' snapped[9] Jeremy. 'I was seen outside Lady Jane's room on the night of the murder.'

1. prise
2. la balance
3. inscrivit
4. ce que vous faisiez
5. grand bien vous fasse
6. nullement découragée
7. le dos voûté
8. sale fouineur de flic
9. rétorqua sèchement

'Oh, Jeremy. What happened?'

'My father phoned me and told me about her. I got into a silly mess[1] when I was at Oxford and I wanted to make sure she kept her mouth shut. She said if I spent the night with her, she would think about it. Can you imagine? That awful old cow[2].'

Alice tried to withdraw her hand. What if Jeremy had murdered Lady Jane? He looked so odd, older, grimmer[3], and there was a muscle jumping[4] in his left cheek.

Jeremy turned and looked at her. 'It wouldn't have mattered so much[5] if she had written about you,' said Alice timidly. 'I mean, it wasn't so very bad.'

'You don't know anything about it,' snapped Jeremy. In a flat voice[6], he told Alice of his Oxford scandals, although he omitted the fact he was still paying for the support of the barmaid's child.

'I could never have gone in for politics,' he said. He felt shaken with nerves and anger. How stupid he'd been not to have told Hamish the whole thing. He needed a drink ... or something.

He seized Alice suddenly and pulled her down on the bed. 'Oh, Jeremy,' whispered Alice, forgetting that she had thought him a murderer a moment ago, 'do you love me?'

'Yes, yes,' mumbled[7] Jeremy against her hair. He started to unbutton her blouse[8], and Alice was so thrilled and excited that he had confessed his love that she almost enjoyed the next ten minutes.

1. ai eu une embrouille
2. sale conne
3. plus sombre
4. qui tressautait
5. Ça n'aurait pas été si grave
6. D'un ton morne
7. marmonna
8. chemisier

Day Six

Hope not for minde in women[1].
– John Donne

1. N'escompte pas d'esprit chez la femme

Hamish was up very early. He had been unable to sleep. It had been a miserable dinner party. Only Alice had seemed to enjoy herself. Daphne Gore appeared to be haunted by the spirit of Lady Jane in that[2] she had seemed hell-bent on[3] ruining the evening for everyone. Hamish could only be glad young Charlie was not present. The boy was suffering enough from hysterical women in the shape[4] of his mother. Hamish had worn the dark grey suit that he kept for his occasional visits to church, and Daphne Gore had said he looked dressed for a funeral. She had then started to harangue the Roths over the American cruise missiles[5], although it was evident to all that she was merely trying to be bitchy[6] and didn't care much one way or the other[7].

They had all drunk too much, because Amy had the nervous habit of constantly refilling their glasses without waiting for the waiter to come around[8].

And then as the climax to a truly horrible evening, Priscilla had arrived for dinner at the hotel with John Harrington. Harrington was everything Hamish detested in a man. He had a loud, carrying[9] English voice, he fussed over[10] the wine,

2. dans la mesure où
3. bien déterminée à
4. en la personne
5. missiles de croisière [à longue portée]
6. essayait juste de faire sa peau de vache
7. n'en avait au fond pas grand-chose à faire
8. le passage du serveur
9. sonore
10. chipotait sur

he criticized the food. He had beautifully tailored clothes, a square, immaculately barbered chin, a tanned rugged[1] face, and crinkly[2] brown hair. And he made Priscilla laugh.

1. rude, viril et bien bronzé
2. ondulés

Hamish decided to take his boat out and try to catch some mackerel. He wandered down to[3] the beach and untied the painter[4] of his rowing boat. It was then that he saw the small figure of Charlie Baxter wistfully[5] watching him.

3. partit d'un pas nonchalant vers
4. amarre
5. d'un air mélancolique

'Want to go out with me?' called Hamish, and Charlie scampered down[6] the beach.

6. descendit en courant sur

'What are you doing out so early, laddie[7]?' asked Hamish. 'It isn't even six o'clock yet.'

7. bonhomme

'I wanted to get out,' said Charlie. 'My mother won't mind. I often go out early for a walk. Things are pretty rough[8]. I want to stay on with Auntie, and Mother wants me to go back.'

8. Ça va plutôt mal

'Maybe I'll have a wee word with her,' said Hamish. 'Hop in[9] and keep still[10].'

9. Monte
10. tiens-toi tranquille

Charlie obeyed, sitting in the boat while Hamish pushed it out into the still waters of Lochdubh. The sun was just peeping over the horizon. The water was like glass, and the sky above was cloudless. 'Looks as if it's going to be a hot day,' said Hamish, climbing in and taking the oars. He rowed them steadily out into the loch.

'Where are we going?' asked Charlie.

'To catch mackerel[11]. Dead easy[12].'

'What with?'

'A spinner[13]. I'll stop in a bit and show you how to do it.'

11. des maquereaux
12. Hyper fastoche
13. cuillère [leurre qui tourne dans l'eau]

'Are we going right out to sea?'

'No, just a bit further.'

Charlie relapsed into silence, hanging over the side of the boat and staring at the sunlight dancing on the water.

Hamish at last shipped the oars[1] and picked up a reel[2] of stout twine[3] with several hooks and silver spinners attached to it.

'Do we bait the hooks[4]?' asked Charlie with interest.

'No, the spinners do the trick[5]. Mackerel will go for[6] nearly anything. That's why they're sometimes called the scavengers[7] of the sea. Just unwind[8] the line and let it trail[9] out behind the boat,' said Hamish.

He began to row again, this time slowly and easily, shipping the oars from time to time.

Behind them, smoke began to rise from the chimneys of the village, and the twisted grotesque forms of the mountains stood out sharp against the clear sky.

'Stop the boat,' shrieked Charlie suddenly. 'I think there's something biting.'

'Pull in the line,' said Hamish, shipping the oars. Charlie wound[10] the line in feverishly. 'There's fish on the end,' he said. 'Fish!'

'Pull them in, there's a good lad[11].'

Charlie jerked[12] the line and hooks, spinners, fish and all crashed behind him in the boat.

'There's four mackerel,' said Charlie as Hamish expertly dislodged the hooks and killed the fish. 'Can we try again?'

'Och, no,' said Hamish. 'We'll just keep to[13] what we can eat. Ready for breakfast?'

'You mean we'll *cook* them?'

'Of course we will. It's too early to wake your mother, so we'll drop a note[14] through the door to tell her where you are.'

Looking more childlike than Hamish had seen him before, Charlie smiled shyly and said, 'You

1. rentra les rames
2. bobine
3. grosse ficelle
4. Est-ce qu'on met un appât sur les hameçons
5. suffisent
6. gobent
7. charognards
8. Déroule
9. traîner
10. rembobina
11. c'est bien, mon gars
12. tira d'un coup sec sur
13. On va s'en tenir à
14. on va glisser un mot

know, everything's really so much better now that terrible woman has gone. I wish I could stay here.'

'But your auntie has just come up for the summer.'

'I overheard her say that she would stay on and put me to the school in Strathbane if my mother would leave me[1].'

'And you would like that?'

'Yes, Mr Macbeth. There's that Mr Blair waiting for you on the beach,' said Charlie. 'Does that mean we can't cook our catch?'

'No, whatever happens, we'll have time to eat.'

But Hamish privately thought it must be something very important to get Mr Blair out of his bed so early.

'Well, we've got[2] our man,' said Mr Blair after Hamish had pulled up his boat on the beach. 'While you were out enjoying yourself and playing with the weans[3], I got a call from Scotland Yard. Major Peter Frame was arrested two years ago for trying to strangle the secretary of the Buffers Club in Pall Mall[4]. What d'you make of that[5]?'

'I would say it was still not proof the man strangled Lady Jane.'

'Yes, well that's why you're a village bobby and I'm not. The man threatened her in front of witnesses.'

'Have you arrested him?'

'Not yet. He's just helping us with our inquiries[6].'

'I gather he's got a fine war record[7].'

'Not him,' sneered[8] Blair. 'That's something else we found out about him. He looks old enough, God knows, but he's only fifty-four. He never was in the war, he never saw any action[9]. He was a major in the Educational Corps in some unit down in Lincolnshire.'

1. était d'accord
2. on tient
3. mioches
4. [quartier chic de Londres]
5. Que dites-vous de ça
6. On l'interroge pour complément d'enquête
7. de beaux états de service durant la guerre
8. ricana
9. n'a jamais été au feu

'I am sure Lady Jane knew that,' said Hamish slowly.

'We're managing fine without your help, although instead of wasting your time fishing, you might see to your duties. That prick[1], Halburton-Smythe, was howling down the phone last night about some poacher.'

'I will see to it,' said Hamish, but Blair was already striding away.

Hamish stood looking after the detective, lost in thought. What if there had been a Lady Jane present at one of the other fishing classes? Would the same lies and petty snobberies have risen to the surface as well?

Charlie tugged his sleeve[2]. 'I rather like Major Frame,' he said. 'He's a bit of an ass[3], but he's jolly kind[4].'

'Let's leave a note for your mother,' said Hamish, 'and then we will have our breakfast.' But before he cooked breakfast, he phoned Angus MacGregor, a layabout[5] who lived on the other side of the village.

'Is that yourself?' said Hamish. 'Aye, well, Angus, your sins[6] have found you out[7] because I am coming to arrest you after I have had my breakfast.'

Charlie listened with interest as the phone squawked[8].

'Nonsense,' said Hamish at last. 'Havers[9]. You bought that new rifle[10] and it is well known that you could not hit the barn door. I will be over[11] soon with the handcuffs[12].'

Hamish put the phone down and grinned at Charlie.

'If he knows you are going to arrest him he might run away,' said the boy, round-eyed[13].

1. sale type
2. tira sur sa manche
3. bêta
4. drôlement gentil
5. bon à rien
6. péchés
7. t'ont trahi
8. braillait
9. Sottises [écossais]
10. fusil
11. arrive
12. menottes
13. éberlué

'That's just what he will do,' said Hamish, leading the way to the kitchen. 'We'd best hide out in here, for they'll be along[1] with the major any moment. Yes, you see Angus has the[2] wife and three children and it would not be right to take their useless father away from them to prison, so he will probably go to Aberdeen for a bit and he will return when he thinks[3] I have forgotten about it. But he will not be trying to bag[4] one of the colonel's stags[5] again.'

After a sustaining breakfast of mackerel dipped in oatmeal[6] and fried in butter, Hamish accompanied Charlie home and was shortly closeted[7] with Mrs Baxter for what seemed to the anxiously awaiting Charlie a very long time indeed.

When he emerged, he merely ruffled[8] Charlie's curls and took himself off[9].

He wandered along to the hotel to learn what the fishing school intended to do for the day. He found them all, with the exception of young Charlie and the major, seated in the lounge, getting a lecture on the ways[10] of trout and salmon from John.

The Roths, Daphne, Jeremy and Alice were in high spirits[11]. Even John Cartwright was cracking[12] jokes. All had heard of the major's 'arrest', and all were determined to believe him guilty.

'It seems as if Mr Blair won't be needing to grill us[13] anymore,' said John, 'so we can go back to Loch Alsh and get some good fishing.' As they all left the hotel, Hamish noticed that Jeremy had an arm around Alice's shoulders.

Alice had spent the whole night in Jeremy's bed. She felt light-headed[14] with debility[15], happiness and relief[16]. It was awful to have to go to the Cartwrights' estate car with Charlie who had just

1. vont arriver
2. sa
3. pensera
4. de choper
5. cerfs
6. pané à la farine d'avoine
7. en tête à tête
8. ébouriffa juste
9. s'en fut
10. mœurs
11. de très bonne humeur
12. racontait
13. nous cuisiner
14. étourdie
15. de faiblesse
16. de soulagement

joined the party and leave Jeremy with Daphne, but he had promised to spend the day with her, Alice, and now she was sure he was on the point of proposing[1].

The nightmare[2] was over. The murderer had been arrested. Alice, like the rest, had not really believed that 'helping the police with their inquiries' stuff. She began to wonder if she would have to give evidence[3] at the trial[4]. That would be exciting since she no longer had anything to fear from the newspapers.

The countryside now looked friendly. Heather blazed purple down[5] the flanks of the mountain sides, and a peregrine falcon soared high[6] in the wind currents in the sky above.

And then a little cloud began to appear on the sunny horizon of Alice's mind. The clean, clear air was invigorating. Set against it[7], the dark, blanket-tussled writhings[8] of the previous night seemed grimy[9]. Then, again, he had not waited for her but had rushed off for breakfast, leaving her to make her own way down[10]. There had been no long days of exchanged glances and holding hands. Alice shrugged and tried to feel worldly-wise[11]. Wham bang, thank you, ma'am,[12] was reality. All men were the same.

But her heart lifted when she climbed out of the car and Jeremy grinned and winked at her[13].

Her heart soared again when Daphne failed to lure[14] Jeremy to join her in fishing at the mouth of the river. 'I'll stay here with Alice,' he said. 'She seems to be lucky.'

There it was – tantamount[15] to an open declaration of love.

Jeremy and Alice fished amiably, if unsuccessfully, up until lunchtime. Alice had lost her

1. faire sa demande
2. cauchemar
3. témoigner
4. au procès
5. Le pourpre de la bruyère blamboyait sur
6. faucon pèlerin s'élevait très haut
7. Par contraste
8. contorsions en chambre
9. sordides
10. descendre toute seule
11. pleine d'expérience
12. Un petit coup vite fait
13. lui fit un clin d'œil
14. les charmes de Daphne ne purent convaincre
15. l'équivalent

fishing fever. All she wanted was Jeremy's company. But when they broke for lunch, it transpired that Jeremy was still gripped by the[1] desire to catch a fish.

1. en proie au

'Where's Daphne?' he said crossly. 'I haven't even had a nibble[2]. Maybe I should have gone with her.'

2. l'ombre d'une prise

'She's at the head of the loch by the river,' said Heather.

'If she's still fishing after this time, she must have got something,' said Jeremy. 'I think I'll go and look.'

Heather glanced at Alice's dismal[3] face. 'Finish your sandwiches,' she said placidly, 'and we'll all go and look. Oh, drat[4], here's the village bobby. Imagine travelling all this way just to scrounge[5] a sandwich ...'

3. atterré

4. flûte

5. grappiller

Hamish sauntered up, red hair and shiny uniform gleaming in the sun.

'How is Major Frame?' asked Alice. 'Have they taken him off to Strathbane?'

'No, I thought he would be here by now,' said Hamish.

'Here?' shrieked everyone.

'Aye,' said Hamish. 'They had to let him go. That business where he was said to strangle[6] the club secretary was a bit of a storm in a teacup[7]. The good major was drunk and the secretary objected to the fact that the major hadn't paid his membership fee[8] and seemed to have no intention of doing so. One word led to another and the major attacked the secretary. Several members of the club pulled them apart[9]. The police were called, but no charges pressed[10]. You can't send a man to prison for a murder just because he got drunk and bad-tempered a wee while ago.'

6. était censé avoir étranglé

7. tempête dans un verre d'eau

8. cotisation

9. les ont séparés

10. il n'y a pas eu de poursuites

'But if he isn't the murderer,' said Alice, 'who is?'

They all looked at each other in dismay[1].

Then a faint scream reached their ears, borne on[2] the light breeze.

'Daphne!' said John Cartwright, lurching to his feet. They all scrambled for[3] the loch and waded in[4]. Hamish took off his boots, socks and trousers and, cutting a ridiculous figure[5] in his tunic, cap and underpants, waded into the water after them.

As they ploughed through the shallow loch towards the river, they saw Daphne. Her rod was bent, her line was taut[6], and she called over her shoulder, 'Keep clear[7]! I want to get this one myself.' They all moved forward, however, watching as she battled with the leaping, plunging fish.

'She'll lose it,' said Heather. 'John, do something.'

'Not me,' said John. 'She wouldn't thank me for any help. Just look at her face!'

Daphne seemed to have aged[8]. Her mouth was clamped tight with deep grooves of strain down either side[9].

Half an hour passed. Even Hamish, ridiculous in his half dress, stayed where he was. Daphne had played[10] her salmon – for a salmon it was[11] – into the shallow water.

With an exclamation of rage, she suddenly threw her rod down and leapt on the salmon, falling on it in a sort of rugby tackle[12]. Then she rose from the frothing[13], swirling water, clutching[14] the salmon to her bosom[15].

She *ran* to the shore, stumbled up the bank, fell and cut her knee, stood up with a great tear[16] across one wader, ran again until she collapsed on the tussocky grass[17] with the writhing[18] fish under her.

1. avec consternation
2. porté par
3. se ruèrent vers
4. entrèrent dans l'eau
5. l'air ridicule
6. très tendue
7. N'approchez pas
8. vieilli
9. La tension nerveuse lui serrait les lèvres, creusant de profondes rides aux commissures
10. fait passer [en le fatiguant peu à peu]
11. car c'était bien un saumon
12. comme dans un plaquage au rugby
13. écumante
14. serrant
15. contre son sein
16. déchirure
17. touffes d'herbe
18. frétillant

They all scrambled to shore. 'Let me get the hook out and kill it for you,' called John.

'Don't you dare[1],' said Daphne. 'That's going to be my pleasure.'

They were saved from watching Daphne kill her fish by a yell from the opposite shore. The major was standing there in full fishing rig[2].

He waded across to join them.

Hamish watched his approach. He would have expected the major to bluster[3], to scream about the disgrace of being taken along to the police station, but the major's eyes were riveted[4] on Daphne and her salmon.

'By Jove, where did you get that?'

'Over there,' panted Daphne.

'What fly were you using?'

'A Gore Inexpressible[5]. It's one of my father's inventions.'

'Where does he fish?'

'He's got an estate[6] in Argyll[7] he uses in the summer. Wouldn't even let me try, which is why I came here. I want one hundred photos to send to him.'

Heather opened her mouth to sympathize with the major over his treatment at the hands of the police, but he was already back in the water, a fanatical gleam[8] in his eye, his whole concentration bent on the foaming water.

Then she noticed the still[9], intent[10] sort of look on Jeremy's face. Oh dear, thought Heather. That remark of Daphne's about her father having an estate in Argyll really got home[11]. Poor Alice.

'Coo-ee!'

The slim figure of Priscilla Halburton-Smythe could be seen on the opposite shore. 'Mr Macbeth,' she called.

1. N'y pensez pas
2. en tenue de pêche de pied en cap
3. se serait attendu à le voir fulminer
4. rivés
5. indicible
6. domaine
7. [région de l'ouest de l'Écosse]
8. lueur
9. figé
10. concentré
11. lui a fait de l'effet

'Better put your pants[1] on first,' said Marvin Roth to Hamish, but Hamish was already off and wading across the loch in Priscilla's direction.

'Sheesh!' said Marvin. 'She'll scream the place down[2] when she sees him.'

'Your Highlander[3] is very prudish[4] about some things,' said Heather. 'But any state of undress[5] doesn't seem to embarrass them, and I'm sure the Halburton-Smythes have become used to it by now.'

'You're all wet,' giggled[6] Priscilla as Hamish waded out. 'I came rushing over to tell you that Daddy's in a fearful rage. He's had collect calls[7] from the States and from London. Lucy Hanson, the secretary, accepted the calls and messages thinking they were something to do[8] with the estate. I asked Daddy to give them to me to pass on[9], but he won't[10].'

'Maybe if we went now we could take a look in the office when he's not around,' said Hamish, water dripping down his long, red-haired legs.

'We might be lucky. Everyone's out in the garden having tea. Haven't you got anything to dry yourself with? You look like something out of a *Carry On* film[11].'

'If we open the windows of the car, I'll dry soon enough,' said Hamish. 'It is just my legs that are wet. The water did not reach my bum[12].' 'We'll take my car,' said Priscilla, 'then I'll drop you off back here. Anyone catch anything?'

So as they drove along, Hamish told her about Daphne's catch, and Priscilla threw back her head and laughed. She was wearing a simple pink cotton sheath[13], and her slim, tanned legs ended in white sandals with thin straps and very high heels. Her legs were like satin. Hamish

1. pantalon
2. va hurler à la mort
3. Le montagnard écossais
4. pudibond
5. nudité
6. s'esclaffa
7. des appels en PCV
8. en lien
9. et que je vous les transmette
10. refuse
11. avez l'air de sortir d'une comédie bas de gamme
12. derrière
13. robe fourreau

wondered if she shaved them or whether they were naturally smooth. He wondered what it would be like to run[1] a hand down – or up – all that silky smoothness[2].

'Stop dreaming,' said Priscilla. 'We're here.'

'I should have put my trousers on at a quiet bit down the road,' said Hamish. 'But there doesn't seem to be anyone about[3] so I'll just pop them on[4].'

'Well, hurry up. Oh, lor[5]!'

Hamish had got his socks on and had his trousers draped[6] on the gravel drive[7] preparatory to putting them on when Colonel and Mrs Halburton-Smythe and five guests including John Harrington rounded the corner of the house.

The colonel goggled at[8] Hamish, who stood frozen, one leg in his trousers and one out. He's going to say, 'What the hell is the meaning of this?' thought Hamish.

'What the hell is the meaning of this?' screamed the colonel. Mrs Halburton-Smythe, who was younger than the colonel and had rather pretty, if faded[9], blonde good looks[10], shouted, 'Come here this minute[11], Priscilla.'

Priscilla thought wildly[12] of the crazy explanations about Daphne's salmon and said hurriedly, 'I'll tell you about it[13] later. Get in the car, Mr Macbeth.'

The colonel started his wrathful advance[14].

Hamish leapt into the car, still half in and half out of his trousers. Priscilla jumped in the other side and they fled off[15] before the colonel could reach them.

'Now I'm for it[16],' said Priscilla gloomily. 'He will never listen, you know, which is why no one ever really tells him anything.'

1. glisser
2. douceur soyeuse
3. là on dirait qu'il n'y a personne
4. vais l'enfiler vite fait
5. zut
6. étalé
7. allée de gravier,
8. roula des yeux ronds en voyant
9. quoique fanée
10. beauté blonde
11. immédiatement
12. frénétiquement
13. vous expliquerai
14. s'approchait, l'air furibond
15. prirent la fuite
16. Mon compte est bon

Hamish wriggled into his trousers[1]. 'And what will you tell your young man? Your father told me – warned me off[2] in fact – that you were about to become engaged[3].'

'I suppose I'd better get engaged to someone,' said Priscilla, concentrating on her driving and therefore[4] missing the look of pain on her companion's face. 'After all, they did take me to London to do the Season[5] and a fat lot of good that was[6]. It cost them a lot of money. All the other girls seemed content to marry someone suitable[7]. My friend, Sarah, was wild about this chap[8], but she married someone else. She said as she walked up to the altar, she thought, "I wish it could have been so-and-so[9]," but she's got a baby now and seems pretty happy.' 'I should think it would be hell to be married to someone you didn't love,' said Hamish, his eyes fixed on the road ahead.

'Really? One never thinks of bobbies as being romantic somehow,' said Priscilla carelessly[10], and the drive back continued in silence. 'Tell your father I caught his poacher,' said Hamish, 'or rather he left Lochdubh before I could arrest him, but Colonel Halburton-Smythe will not be troubled by that poacher again.'

'That might calm him down. I suppose you really have to get those messages. Look, you'd better sneak around[11] about midnight and I'll let you in. I'll try to get them out of the desk for you.'

Hamish nodded and raised his hand in a sort of salute as she drove away. He turned his attention to the fishing party. Alice was sitting by the shore of the loch, plaiting a wreath[12] of wild flowers, like some modern-day Ophelia[13], while Jeremy and Daphne could be seen out in the boat, talking eagerly[14]. There was no sign of the Roths or the

1. se tortilla pour enfiler son pantalon
2. à titre d'avertissement
3. vous fiancer
4. par conséquent
5. [pour la haute société]
6. ça n'a pas servi à grand-chose
7. un parti convenable
8. folle d'un type
9. Untel
10. avec insouciance
11. revenir discrètement
12. à tresser une couronne
13. [infortunée fiancée d'Hamlet]
14. avec animation

Cartwrights. Hamish took off his tunic and, using it as a pillow, stretched his long, lanky length[1] out on the grass. He ran[2] the whole fishing party through his brain, remembering incidents, remembering expressions, remembering what Lady Jane had said. After a time, they all became jumbled together[3] in his head as he fell asleep.

The noise of the fishing party packing up for the day awoke him. The major had caught a salmon, not quite as big as Daphne's, but big enough to make him look as if he had just found the Holy Grail[4].

Charlie came rushing up. 'What did you say to my mother, Mr Macbeth?'

'There's no use me telling you now, laddie, in case things don't work out[5]. Just say your prayers. Hop in and I'll take you home.'

So Alice travelled back with the Cartwrights, worried and lost. If only Jeremy would sleep with her that evening, then she would be sure.

Hamish found Blair waiting for him on his return. The detective was setting out for the hotel for another round of interrogation. Blair was in a fury because he had been so sure at first of the major. He took that fury out[6] on Hamish, calling him lazy, half-witted[7], and useless, while Hamish stood stolidly to attention[8], his mind obviously elsewhere.

Blair was also at his worst[9] with the members of the fishing party that evening. They huddled together[10] at dinner, all now wishing they could go home. Blair had said that they might leave on the Sunday morning but that they could expect further calls[11] from the police when they got home.

No one even had the heart to raise a smile at Marvin Roth's appearance. The American had

1. carcasse dégingandée
2. passa en revue
3. se mélangèrent
4. saint Graal
5. au cas où ça ne marcherait pas
6. se défoula
7. débile
8. stoïquement au garde-à-vous
9. plus odieux que jamais
10. se serraient les uns contre les autres
11. s'attendre à d'autres visites

arrived at dinner in full Highland dress, from plaid and kilt to skean-dhu[1] in his stocking top[2].

Hamish decided to pass the evening hours by going for a long walk. There was no hope of using the phone in his office, since Blair had announced his intention of staying there himself most of the night to sift through[3] the evidence[4] again and make phone calls.

Alice waited in her room after dinner. And waited.

Jeremy was drinking with Daphne in the bar. At last, he escorted Daphne to her room and leaned against the door post and smiled at her. 'Are you inviting me in?' he asked.

'No,' laughed Daphne. 'Not tonight, Napoleon. I've got a headache.'

Jeremy stood frowning after she had shut the door. Anxiety gnawed at him[5] despite the amount of gin he had drunk. He went slowly along to a room further along the corridor and rapped[6] on the door.

'Open up, Alice,' he said. 'It's me.'

Hamish found his steps leading back to the scene of the murder. He shone his torch here and there among the bushes, not much hoping to find anything, since the police had already been over the ground very thoroughly[7].

He suddenly switched off his torch and stood very still. Up above the pool, in the little glade[8] where the fishing party had sat after the discovery of the murder, a twig[9] snapped[10]. He began to move very silently in the direction of the glade, walking in the long grass beside the path so that his feet would make no sound. There was something ancient and eerie[11] about the Highland

1. [petit couteau traditionnel]
2. en haut de la chaussette
3. passer au peigne fin
4. preuves
5. le rongeait
6. frappa légèrement
7. soigneusement
8. clairière
9. brindille
10. craqua
11. d'inquiétant

silence. The night was very still. He stopped at the edge of the glade. A small moon shone down through the trees. Bars[1] of light cut across the scene.

Moving through the flickering bars of light, crouched[2] low like some jungle animal, was Amy Roth. Her restless hands searched[3] the grass.

'Good evening, Mrs Roth,' said Hamish.

Amy stood up slowly and turned to face him, her face a white disc in the shadow.

'Who is it?' she whispered.

'Constable Macbeth.'

'Oh.' She gave a little laugh and brushed nervously at her clothes. 'I lost my lighter[4]. It's gold. I thought I might have left it here.'

'A funny time and a scary place to come looking for a lighter,' said Hamish. 'Why are you *really* here?'

'It's late,' she said, moving towards him. 'I'm going back to the hotel.'

'How long is it since you have suspected your husband of the murder?' asked Hamish.

Amy put her hands to her face. 'Marvin can be so violent,' she whispered. 'But he couldn't ... surely ...' With a gasp[5], she thrust past him[6] and fled down the path. Hamish watched her go and shook his head. He had only been guessing, but his remark seemed to have struck gold[7]. He shone his torch around the glade and then decided to examine the ground about the pool before finishing his search. He searched and searched about the ground and the bushes when something caught his eye. He forced his way into the undergrowth and shone his torch. A strand[8] of blue material was caught on a thorn[9]. Strange that the forensic men had missed it.

1. Des rayons
2. tapie
3. fouillaient
4. briquet
5. hoquet
6. le bouscula pour passer
7. tapé dans le mille
8. lambeau
9. épine

He carefully took it off the thorn and examined it. It was of a powder blue colour and made of acrylic. He remembered Alice had been wearing a blue trouser suit on the first day of the fishing class.

He sat down thoughtfully[1] by the pool and turned the scrap of material[2] over between finger and thumb. But someone very recently had been wearing just such a[3] colour. His hand suddenly clenched[4], and he was seized with a feeling of fear and dread.

'Oh no,' he whispered.

1. pensivement
2. bout de tissu
3. exactement cette
4. se crispa

Day Seven

1. Ce qui distingue
2. capacité à fatiguer
3. de bonne taille
4. avec
5. standard ou léger
6. à bonne distance
7. trajet
8. hésitait à
9. trouver tout seul son chemin
10. nullement provocant
11. tenue
12. à bavasser
13. truc abracadabrant
14. la sténo de Miss Abrutie

The test of[1] *an experienced angler is his ability to play*[2] *a good-sized*[3] *fish on*[4] *average or light*[5] *equipment.*

– Gilmer G. Robinson, *Fly Casting*

At three minutes after midnight, Hamish parked his car well away[6] from the Halburton-Smythe castle and finished his journey[7] on foot. He was wondering whether to[8] risk trying the door and finding his own way about[9] when it opened and Priscilla whispered, 'Hurry up, before we wake the whole house.'

She led the way up flights of stairs to her bedroom. She was wearing a white cotton nightgown and negligee, very unrevealing[10], but Constable Macbeth felt he had never seen such a seductive-looking outfit[11] in his life.

'Now,' said Priscilla, sitting down on the bed and patting the space beside her, 'I managed to get into the estates office when they were all jawing[12] about your inquiries at dinner. Mummy believed my story. She said it was just the sort of hare-brained thing[13] you *would* do. There are the messages, but they're in Miss Dimwit's shorthand[14].'

Hamish took the notes. 'I do shorthand myself, Miss Halburton-Smythe. But whether I could read this. Yes, I think ...'

'Are you asleep, Prissie? I want to talk to you.'

'Daddy,' squeaked[1] Priscilla. 'Into bed, quick, and under the blankets. As far over by the wall as you can get.'

Hamish was fortunately not in uniform. The night was warm so he was wearing a checked[2] cotton shirt and an old pair of flannels.

He leapt into bed, under the blankets, and crouched down[3]. Priscilla got in beside him and leaned against the pillows. 'Come in!' she called.

Hamish lay very still with his head under the blankets. His face was pressed against Priscilla's thigh[4]. He tried to move it away and she slapped[5] the top of the bedclothes[6] as a warning to him to lie still[7].

Colonel Halburton-Smythe came into the room. He sat down on the edge of the bed, and Priscilla shifted[8] to make room for him. She was jammed[9] against Hamish, who felt like groaning[10].

'Look, pet,[11] the Harringtons might leave tomorrow for the simple reason that you won't come to the point[12],' he heard the colonel say. 'Harrington's a fine young chap. It's not as if you're in love with anyone. You can't go on turning down[13] one fellow after another.'

'I could get a job, Daddy.'

'Nonsense. Marriage and children's the only career for a woman. What will I tell the Harringtons?'

'Tell them anything,' yawned[14] Priscilla 'I'm so beastly tired, Daddy. I promise I'll be nice to John tomorrow if you'll just go away.'

'Very well,' said the colonel. 'But don't keep him waiting around too long.'

At last, to Hamish's intense relief[15], he heard the door close. Priscilla threw back the bedclothes and looked down at Hamish's ruffled red hair.

1. glapit
2. à carreaux
3. se ratatina
4. la cuisse
5. claqua
6. couvre-lit
7. pour lui enjoindre de ne pas bouger
8. se décala
9. écrasée
10. eut envie de grogner
11. mon chou,
12. ne te décides pas
13. continuer à rejeter
14. bâilla
15. soulagement

'You look quite sweet[1] without that horrible uniform on,' said Priscilla. 'You must have been nearly suffocated. Your face is all red and you're breathing like a grampus[2].'

'I'm all right,' said Hamish, sitting up with an effort. 'Let me have a look at those notes.'

Priscilla took them out from under her pillow and handed them to him. He frowned as he studied them, and then his face sharpened[3]. 'I've got to use the phone,' he said.

'You look terrible,' said Priscilla. 'What is it? Why can't you use the phone at that police station of yours?'

'Blair's there and probably all night. Can I use the one in the estates office?'

'Yes, so long as no one discovers you.' Priscilla felt rather sulky[4] and wondered why. 'I wouldn't have thought you were so keen on[5] your job.'

'Aye,' said Hamish, climbing over her[6] to get out of bed. 'I'll just creep down the stairs. No one will hear me.'

'Good night,' said Priscilla crossly[7].

Hamish smiled down at her as she lay against the pillows. 'Thank you for all you have done, Miss Halburton-Smythe.' He bent suddenly and kissed her on the cheek, turned red as fire, and fled from the room.

'Well, well,' thought Priscilla. She put a hand up to her cheek and stared in a bemused way[8] at the closed door.

Hamish sat beside the phone in the estates office and in his head turned over the names of his many relatives. There was Rory in London, Erchie in New York, Peter in Hong Kong, Jenny in Aylesbury, which was near enough to Oxford ...

1. êtes mignon,
2. soufflez comme un phoque [littéralement, *comme une orque*]
3. regard s'aiguisa
4. grincheuse
5. si intéressé par
6. en l'enjambant
7. avec mauvaise humeur
8. l'air songeur

At last, he picked up the phone and began to dial[1].

A pale dawn was lighting up the sky and the water as Hamish Macbeth wearily made his way along the waterfront. There was something he had to do before he went to sleep and it was something that only duty[2] was prompting him[3] to do. His heart felt heavy, and his lips moved in a soundless Gaelic prayer.

He turned in at a white-painted gate and went around the back of the house to the kitchen door. He rapped loud[4] and long on the glass[5] until he saw a light go on upstairs. He waited, hearing footsteps descending, shuffling footsteps[6] approaching the kitchen door.

The door opened and Tina Baxter stood blinking at him[7] nervously. She clutched a pink woollen dressing gown[8] tightly at her neck. All colour drained[9] from her face.

'Aye, it's me,' said Hamish heavily. 'Mind if I come in?'

She stood aside, and he walked past her into the kitchen. She followed him and sat down at the kitchen table as if her legs could no longer bear her weight.

'I was here earlier,' said Hamish, 'talking to you about young Charlie's future. You were wearing a blue dress.' He took an envelope out of his tunic pocket and extracted the piece of material he had found on the bush beside the pool. 'Is this yours?'

'Yes,' whispered Mrs Baxter. She covered her face with her hands and began to cry.

'I couldn't help it[10],' she sobbed[11]. 'The disgrace[12]. My Charlie's name in the papers. I had to shut her mouth.'

1. composer un numéro
2. le sens du devoir
3. le poussait
4. frappa fort
5. vitre
6. un pas traînant
7. le regardait en clignant des yeux
8. robe de chambre
9. avait disparu
10. n'ai pas pu me retenir
11. sanglota-t-elle
12. honte

Hamish sat down opposite her. His head was beginning to clear[1], and his earlier fright[2] was beginning to recede[3] as common sense took over[4]. The first rays of sun began to warm the kitchen.

'Mrs Baxter,' he said gently. 'Immediately after the murder all the bushes and braes[5] and heather[6] and trees were combed for clues[7] by the forensic boys[8]. It's awfy[9] strange they didn't find this and I did.'

'I did it.' Tina Baxter stared at him, her face working[10].

'Aye, that you did. Not the murder. You cut a bit out of your dress and left it there, hoping someone would find it. So now we'll have another wee chat about Charlie. He's twelve years old. *Twelve years old.* Just think o' that. He's a strong boy but there is no way he could have overpowered[11] a woman of Lady Jane's size. Then there's the lad's character ...'

'It's bad blood[12], bad blood,' said Tina Baxter, her hands clutching and unclutching[13] the material[14] of her dressing gown. 'His father was violent. He threatened to kill me if I didn't give him a divorce.' Her voice was rising hysterically.

'I am thinking,' said Hamish sincerely, 'that you would drive[15] a saint to violence. I feel like striking you myself. Do you know that because of your silly clue-planting[16] you had me thinking[17] you knew that Charlie did it and were trying to fix the blame on yourself[18]? You're a dangerous woman. Now, here's what you are going to do. You are going to leave Charlie here to stay with his aunt and I suggest you go back home and see one o' thae head doctors[19]. You'll drive the bairn[20] mad with all your hysterics.

1. Il commençait à y voir clair
2. frayeur
3. s'estompait
4. prenait le dessus
5. les pentes [écossais]
6. la bruyère
7. passés au peigne fin
8. les gars de la scientifique
9. très [écossais]
10. en grimaçant
11. il aurait été absolument incapable de maîtriser
12. héréditaire
13. aggrippant et lâchant
14. tissu
15. pousseriez
16. vous avez bêtement semé un indice,
17. j'ai cru que
18. de vous attribuer la faute
19. un docteur du ciboulot
20. ce gosse [écossais]

'If you don't do what I say, I will let the newspapers know that you believed your own boy capable of murder and nearly got him accused of it by your clumsiness[1].'

Hamish rose to his feet. 'So think on that, Mrs Baxter. I'll bring mair[2] scandal down on your head than you ever could hae[3] imagined.'

It was the last day of the fishing course[4]. Unless the police requested otherwise[5], Blair would take their home and business addresses and allow them to leave on the Sunday morning. The river Anstey was still closed[6] to them. Heather and John had suggested they fish the Marag.

On returning to the police station, Hamish found that Blair was still asleep. He typed up his notes, studied the results, and then put them to one side. He thought long and carefully about each member of the fishing school. He decided he was being haunted[7] by the scale[8] of the crime. He began to read through his well-thumbed[9] ten-volume edition of *Famous Crimes*. Motives tumbled one after another before his tired eyes[10]. Murder for money, for passion, for revenge. Alcohol or drugs brought out the Hyde side[11] of the character, but no one in the fishing school case[12] drank daily to excess[13] and not one of them had shown any sign of being a drug user. He made one pot after another of strong tea. His dog, Towser, prowled about uneasily[14], stopping to lick his master's hand as if wondering what was keeping him from his bed[15], for Towser liked to stretch out on the bed at Hamish's feet.

'It is all a matter of lack[16] of conscience,' thought Hamish.

1. maladresse
2. [more]
3. [have]
4. stage
5. Sauf instructions contraires de la police
6. interdite d'accès
7. tourmenté
8. ampleur
9. usée
10. défilaient devant ses yeux las
11. côté Mister Hyde
12. affaire
13. à outrance
14. rôdait, mal à l'aise
15. l'empêchait d'aller se coucher
16. manque

By the time the little fishing class was setting out for their last day, Hamish was sound asleep[1], his dog snoring at his feet, and a sheaf[2] of notes clutched to his chest.

He was awakened by Blair shaking his shoulder. 'It's noon,' snarled Blair savagely. 'By God, I'll report you for sheer laziness[3]. I've got a job for you. You'll come along with me to that hotel this evening and you'll take down the addresses of the whole lot of 'em. I don't just mean their home addresses, we've got those. I mean where they work and where they're likely to be visiting.'

'Get out!' said a small, shrill voice behind Blair. The large detective swung around in amazement. Charlie Baxter stood in the doorway clutching a mug of tea. 'This is Constable Macbeth's house,' he said, 'and you've got no right to bully him[4].'

Blair stared at the boy, who was white with anger.

Hamish, who had fallen asleep in the shirt and flannels he had worn the night before, swung his legs quickly out of bed.

'Into the kitchen with you[5], Charlie,' he said. 'What time will you be wanting me at the hotel, sir?'

'Six o'clock,' snapped Blair. 'And tell that kid to mind his manners[6].' He stomped off[7] where he could shortly be heard haranguing MacNab and Anderson in Hamish's office.

'I've prepared breakfast for you, Mr Macbeth,' said Charlie shyly. 'It's on the table.' 'Aye, you've done very well,' said Hamish, tucking into[8] charred[9] bacon and rubbery[10] egg. 'Quite the wee housewife[11]. Aren't you going fishing?'

'I thought you might run up to the Marag with me,' said Charlie. 'You see, I have to thank you.

1. dormait à poings fermés
2. liasse
3. paresse pure et simple
4. le malmener
5. File dans la cuisine
6. mieux se tenir
7. partit lourdement
8. attaquant avec entrain
9. calciné
10. caoutchouteux
11. Une vraie petite fée du logis

Mother left in a rage[1]. I don't know what you said or what Auntie said to her afterwards, but I'm to stay[2].'

'Isn't that the great thing,' smiled Hamish. 'Och, your ma's a decent body[3], but she worries overmuch about everything[4].'

'Perhaps we'll catch the murderer together, Mr Macbeth.'

'We might at that[5]. Wait till I put on my uniform and we'll be off.'

There was a festival air about the fishing school. Even Daphne seemed to have stopped her bitchy behaviour. All of them had come to the conclusion at breakfast that none of them had done it and Lady Jane had probably come across[6] a poacher or some itinerant madman. Tomorrow, they would all return home with a story they could dine out on[7] for years.

Alice drew Hamish aside and showed him a silver and cairngorm[8] ring she was wearing on a string around her neck. 'Jeremy gave this to me,' she said. 'He bought it at the gift shop this morning. I was going to put it on my finger, but he said to keep it secret for the moment.'

'Why?' asked Hamish curiously. 'It is not as if the man is married.'

'Oh, you men are so secretive,' laughed Alice.

'If I were to be married to the lady of my choice,' said Hamish slowly, 'I would shout it from the mountain top[9].'

But Alice only giggled[10] happily and walked away. Hamish went to sit on a rock where he could get a view of everyone in the fishing school and there he stayed for the whole of the day. At last, at five o'clock, he walked up to Heather and said, 'You are all expected in the hotel at six o'clock,

1. furieuse
2. il est prévu que je reste
3. quelqu'un de bien
4. beaucoup trop
5. Mais c'est qu'on pourrait bien
6. croisé
7. qui ferait leurs choux gras
8. de quartz fumé
9. le crierais sur tous les toits
10. gloussa

Mrs Cartwright. They will want to wash and change. Mr Blair wants me to take your names and addresses, and myself will be having a bit of a word[1] with you.'

'All right,' said Heather, looking curiously at Hamish's face. 'I'll get them together.'

'I will go on,' said Hamish, 'and make sure that no other guests are allowed in the lounge.' At the hotel, Hamish found Blair, MacNab and Anderson waiting for him. 'They are coming,' said Hamish, 'and will be in the lounge at six. I am just going to tell Mr Johnson to keep other guests out of the lounge. You see, I am going to find your murderer for you, Mr Blair.'

MacNab sniggered[2], and Jimmy Anderson said, 'You've been reading too many detective stories[3], Hamish. Great detective gathers suspects in the library and unmasks killer.'

'Aye, chust so[4],' said Hamish, walking off.

'He's mad,' growled MacNab. 'I'll tell him to go home and have some black coffee.'

'No,' said Blair. 'Let him get on with it[5]. I want him to make a right fool of himself[6]. I'll have him out of his cushy job[7] in a week.'

And so Hamish found Blair surprisingly mild[8] and cooperative when he returned. Yes. Blair grinned. MacNab would guard the door and Anderson the window.

At last, one by one, the members of the fishing party entered the lounge. Hamish stood with his back to the empty fireplace and waited until they were all seated.

'Before I take down your addresses and send you on your way[9] tomorrow,' he said, 'there's just a few things I have to say.' MacNab stifled[10] a laugh.

1. une petite conversation
2. ricana
3. romans policiers
4. exactement
5. faire
6. qu'il se ridiculise
7. l'aurai fait virer de sa planque
8. doux
9. vous laisse repartir
10. étouffa

'It was a wee bit difficult for me to see at first which one of you had done the murder because you all seemed to have a motive.'

'Get on with it[1].' Daphne Gore yawned. 'I'm dying for a drink.'

'John and Heather Cartwright,' went on Hamish, ignoring the interruption. 'A bad press might have ruined your school, and there was no doubt that Lady Jane meant to give you a bad write-up[2]. You had a letter from friends in Austria telling you how she had managed to ruin *them*. Mr Cartwright lives for this fishing school and Mrs Cartwright lives for her husband. Both could have committed the murder ... or one of them.

'Marvin and Amy Roth ...'

'I'm not going to listen to any more of this,' said Heather. She half rose from her chair, her face flushed with distress, changed her mind, and sat down again, looking not at Hamish, but at her husband.

'Marvin Roth,' said Hamish, 'was involved in a scandal some years ago when he was charged with running sweatshops in the garment district of New York and employing illegal aliens. He did not want his past raked up[3] just when he was set on[4] entering politics, and he guessed from a remark Lady Jane made that she knew all about his past.

'Then Amy Roth. Always talking about being a Blanchard from Augusta, except you aren't a Blanchard by birth. You married Tom Blanchard ten years ago and the marriage only lasted a few weeks, but you kept his name and background. Lady Jane must have known that.'

Marvin polished the top of his bald head.

1. Dépêchez-vous

2. critique incendiaire

3. remonte à la surface

4. décidé à

'Look here,' he said desperately. 'Amy didn't say anything about being a Blanchard by birth, now did you, hon[1]?'

'Oh, yes, she did,' said Daphne. 'Right down to the last mint julep[2].'

'You misheard,' said Marvin, giving Daphne a cold, pale look.

'Then we come to Major Peter Frame,' said Hamish.

'Not again,' said the major, burying his face in his hands.

'You care very much for your reputation as an officer and a gentleman,' said Hamish. 'You have an excitable temper[3] and you were heard to threaten Lady Jane's life. You were never in the war, nor have you a particularly upperclass[4] background. Lady Jane gave you a rough time[5].

'Alice Wilson.' Alice smiled tremulously[6] at Jeremy, who frowned and looked at the door. 'You got into minor trouble as a child and it's plagued you[7] ever since. There was a big reason why you did not want the matter to get out. Perhaps you might have killed because of it.'

Nobody moved, but they seemed to shrink away from Alice.

'I wouldn't,' gasped Alice. 'Jeremy, please ...'

'Charlie Baxter,' went on Hamish. 'Well, you had a bad time[8] with her ladyship[9], and boys of your age can do terrible things under stress.

'Jeremy Blythe. I think you are a ruthless[10], ambitious, selfish man. You messed up[11] two women in your Oxford days and God knows how many more. You want to be elected a member of the Conservative party, and Lady Jane's story, had it appeared[12], would have meant the end of your ambitions.'

1. [honey]
2. Dans les moindres détails de la vie sudiste
3. le sang chaud
4. de la haute société
5. vous a malmené
6. en tremblant
7. ça vous poursuit
8. ça se passait mal
9. Lady Jane
10. sans scrupules
11. vous avez été dégueulasse avec
12. si elle avait été publiée

'This is cruel,' thought Alice wildly. 'He could have taken us aside[1] one at a time[2]. It's like some horrible game of truths, bringing all our skeletons out of the closet.' She looked angrily at Hamish, who was consulting a sheaf of notes. He raised his eyes and looked around the room. 'He doesn't know who did it!' thought Alice with a sudden flash of intuition. 'He's looking for some sign that will betray the murderer.'

'Daphne Gore. Lady Jane knew all about you. I won't go into the details of your background that landed you[3] under psychiatric care[4], but I think you are unbalanced[5] enough to kill someone, given enough[6] stress.'

There was a shocked silence. 'If your little game is over, Macbeth,' said Blair, 'we'll get those addresses and ...'

Hamish ignored him.

'Now we had one clue, a torn corner of a photograph with part of the legend BUY BRIT— in one corner. At first I thought it might be part of an old Buy British poster. The fragment also shows the top of a head with something sparkly on it like a tiara. I made a lot of phone calls and found out at last what the legend really read[7].

'It runs[8] BUY BRITTELS BEER – a kind of beer that is sold in America.'

'Never heard of it,' said Marvin Roth.

'Not many people have,' said Hamish. 'It was made locally by a small firm controlled by the Mafia in the Red Hook section[9] of Brooklyn. It was so strong the locals said[10] it was made out of all the bodies that didn't end up[11] in the East River[12]. It was a bit of luck I found that out. Mrs Roth had muttered[13] something about Red Hook, but at the time, I thought she must be talking about

1. nous prendre à part
2. un par un
3. vous a menée
4. en soins psychiatriques
5. déséquilibrée
6. à partir d'un certain niveau de
7. ce qui était réellement écrit dans cette légende
8. dit [en fait]
9. quartier
10. que, d'après les gens du coin,
11. ne finissaient pas
12. [détroit entre Brooklyn et Manhattan]
13. marmonné

something to do with the fishing. It was only later I remembered Red Hook was a district in Brooklyn. I have a cousin, Erchie, who lives in Red Hook and I phoned him up. He said it was sold in small Mafia gambling clubs[1].

'He neffer[2] heard of Amy Blanchard or Amy Roth, but he had heard of an Amy a whiles back[3] who was a stripper[4], Amy not being a usual name in the Italian section. Now Lady Jane had been in the States, no doubt digging up what dirt she could[5]. Lady Jane was content to wait until her column appeared to see the rest of you[6] suffering or to imagine your suffering. But Amy caught her on the raw[7]. She arranged to meet Mrs Roth in the woods. There she showed her a photograph of Amy the stripper, wearing very little except a spangled headdress[8]. You, Mrs Roth, have very little in the way of a[9] conscience. This is something I *feel* about you, rather than something I definitely know. It came on me[10] bit by bit. The look in the back of your eyes always had a certain steady calculating hardness no matter what you were saying. So you strangled her and then you dragged the body to the pool. You wanted something to weight[11] the body and so you went down to the beach and found some old rusty chain. As soon as you had pushed her into the pool, you felt safe. You then returned to her room and destroyed all her notes and papers. Your husband would never know you were a Brooklyn stripper who sold her favours[12].'

Good God, thought Heather Cartwright wildly. Do people still talk about women selling their favours?

Amy Roth sat very still, her eyes lowered.

1. clubs de jeu
2. [never]
3. y a un moment de ça
4. strip-teaseuse
5. à débusquer un maximum de ragots
6. vous voir tous
7. l'a piquée au vif
8. coiffure pailletée
9. n'êtes guère encombrée de
10. m'est apparu
11. lester
12. ses charmes

Marvin lumbered up[1] and sat on the arm of his wife's chair and put a hand on her shoulder and gave it a comforting squeeze.

'You're talking shit[2],' grated Marvin. 'I won't believe what you said about Amy. I'll tell you something else. She knows I love her. She knows that I wouldn't give a damn about[3] her past. Mine ain't so lily white[4]. Where's your proof?'

'She was seen,' said Hamish. 'There is this poacher, Angus MacGregor ...'

His voice trailed away[5] as Amy raised her eyes and looked at him. Her eyes had lost their soft, cow-like expression. They were as flat and as hard as two stones.

'You did it, didn't you?' said Hamish.

Amy Roth moistened[6] her lips.

'Yes,' she said flatly.

'And when you said you thought your husband had done it and you were frightened he had left something incriminating behind, you were really frightened *you* had left something.'

'Yes,' said Amy again in that dreadful flat voice.

Marvin's face was white and working with[7] emotion. Tears started to his eyes. 'You're making her say all this.' There was a long silence. 'Amy,' pleaded Marvin, 'if you did it, you did it for me. Well, the hell with[8] politics. I wasn't ever sold on[9] the idea anyway.'

'That was not the reason, was it, Amy?' said Hamish.

'I guess not,' she said in a dull voice. She stretched her fingers and looked at them thoughtfully. 'She messed with me[10], that's all. I don't like no one messing with me.'

1. se leva lourdement
2. dites des conneries
3. m'en foutrais de
4. n'est pas blanc-bleu
5. s'éteignit
6. humecta
7. tiraillée d'
8. au diable
9. fana de
10. m'a cherchée

And as Anderson and MacNab closed in on her[1], she gave her husband an apologetic[2] little smile.

Hamish leaned on the harbour wall, keeping his eyes fixed on the sea. He felt immeasurably tired. He did not want to see Amy dragged out[3] to the police car. She would be taken to the women's prison at Strathbane.

He waited a long time while cars came and went. Then he heard Blair's voice behind him. 'That was a neat bit of work[4], Constable. I suppose you're laughing your head off[5]. MacNab and Anderson have taken her to Strathbane with the rest of my men. I'm just about to follow. Fine reading it will make[6] for my superiors. Case solved[7] by the village bobby.'

'Och, no,' said Hamish soothingly[8]. 'It was yourself that pointed the way. I will not be taking any credit[9].'

'Why did you keep this poacher witness[10] up your sleeve[11]? It worked the trick[12].'

'I chust made that up[13],' said Hamish, lighting a cigarette. 'It was all guesswork[14].'

'*What!*'

'Aye. I just took a chance[15]. You see, Erchie told me that the only[16] Amy he had ever heard of around the Mafia clubs away back was a young stripper. He was not sure it was the same person, at all, at all. I just thought I would chance it.'

'But what if you had been wrong?'

'Aye, well, I have no doubt you would have had me out of[17] my job as you were hoping to do. Now Amy had been a bit of a prostitute as well. I noticed that she was always restless[18]. That's the thing about prostitutes. They can cover up

1. se rapprochaient dangereusement d'elle
2. d'excuse
3. emmenée
4. du bon boulot
5. vous marrez bien
6. Vous parlez d'un rapport
7. Affaire résolue
8. d'un ton apaisant
9. ne veux m'attribuer aucun mérite
10. témoin
11. dans votre manche
12. a bien marché
13. l'ai inventé
14. Ce n'étaient que des suppositions
15. risque
16. seule
17. que vous m'auriez fait perdre
18. ne tenait pas en place

the past with a layer of ladylike veneer[1], but they never lose that hunted[2], fidgety[3] air.'

'You having great experience of the breed[4],' said Blair sarcastically.

Hamish blushed. 'No, no. But there was Jessie over[5] in Aberdeen who married that man on the council ... Then there was how Amy behaved at dinner. I couldnae[6] help noticing that she would pour round[7] the wine without waiting for the waiter or the men to do it.'

'Must have been a shock for old Marvin.'

'Aye, it was that.[8] I first started to think it might be her when I looked at her wrists. They're very strong for a woman. But it was her eyelids[9] that clinched the matter[10].'

'Her *eyelids*?'

'They are strained[11] a bit at the corners. I have always noticed that criminal-type women have this feature[12].'

'Mr Roth has gone with her. He's going to get some big-shot lawyer[13].'

'Aye, love is a terrible thing,' said Hamish mournfully[14].

'I think you were damn lucky,' said Blair sourly[15]. 'I can't believe you're not going to take any credit for this.'

Hamish turned and leaned his back against the harbour wall. 'Oh, you can believe it. I have no mind[16] to leave Lochdubh. But if you were to put a little something in your report about my hard-working, if unintelligent[17], help, that would be just fine.'

Blair smiled slowly and clapped Hamish on the shoulder.

'I think we've time for a drink, Hamish,' he said. 'Let's go into the bar.'

1. vernis de savoir-vivre
2. traqué
3. agité
4. cette catégorie
5. là-bas
6. [couldn't]
7. servait
8. Ah çà oui !
9. paupières
10. m'ont donné la certitude
11. étirées
12. trait physique
13. un as du barreau
14. sombrement
15. avec aigreur
16. n'ai nulle intention
17. quoique manquant d'intelligence

Epilogue

1. papotant

2. soulagement que tout ait été éclairci

3. les dépasser sans encombre

4. tant et si bien

5. fanfaronnade

6. stagiaires

7. n'avait annulé

8. éreinté par

9. à l'annulaire [en bague de fiançailles]

10. Je ferais mieux d'y aller

11. de plier bagage

12. joyeusement

Sunday morning. All the survivors chattering[1] and laughing over the breakfast table. Oh, the relief to have it all cleared up[2] and be able to go home. Reporters and photographers waited outside the courtyard of the hotel. But it would be possible to drive straight past them[3]. Only John Cartwright knew that the major had already been out to talk to them. The major was back on form, so much so[4] that he could not bear to admit that the case had been solved by the village constable but merely paused in his bragging[5] to say that he was jolly glad the police had cleared the matter up.

John sighed. The other guests, the new fishing school[6], would be arriving later in the day. Not one had cancelled[7]. They would survive.

Alice smiled radiantly at Jeremy. He had not visited her last night, excusing himself by saying he was all washed up with[8] all the drama of the arrest. She was wearing the ring he had given her on her engagement finger[9].

'Hope to see you all again,' said Major Peter Frame cheerfully. 'Better be on my way[10].'

'I'd better get my traps[11] too,' said Jeremy.

'My suitcase is at the reception so I'll have another cup of coffee and wait for you here,' said Alice sunnily[12]. Jeremy put a hand briefly on her shoulder.

'Better get mine as well,' said Daphne languidly, 'and get my fish out of the freezer. Hope it'll fit[1] in the car.'

The Cartwrights said goodbye and went off to look at equipment for the new members of the fishing school.

Alice sat alone. It was a beautiful day and she sipped[2] her coffee and looked happily out at the sun sparkling[3] on the loch. Perhaps she and Jeremy would return on their honeymoon[4]. All of a sudden she stiffened[5]. Daphne had said something about hoping her fish would fit in the car. Which car? There was really only room[6] for two in Jeremy's sportscar.

She rushed out to reception and grabbed[7] her suitcase and ran out into the courtyard. Jeremy and Daphne were laughing as they tried to find room for Daphne's enormous salmon.

'Jeremy,' cried Alice. 'I thought we were going back together.'

He strolled over to her. 'No, it's only fair I should[8] give Daphne a lift back[9]. After all, we did travel up[10] together.'

'But we're engaged,' shrieked Alice. 'Look! I'm wearing your ring.'

'It was only a present,' mumbled Jeremy. 'I mean, I didn't ask you to marry me, did I?'

'You *slept* with me,' said Alice, beginning to sob. 'I might be pregnant[11].' She threw her arms around Jeremy's neck.

'Good God,' he said. He jerked her arms down[12] and ran for his car. Daphne was already sitting in the passenger seat.

Jeremy climbed in and slammed the door just as Alice ran up. Her hands scrabbled[13] at the window

1. qu'il va tenir
2. sirotait
3. qui étincelait
4. pour leur lune de miel
5. se raidit
6. de la place
7. saisit
8. ce n'est que justice de
9. de remmener Daphne
10. avons fait l'aller
11. enceinte
12. repoussa ses bras d'un coup sec
13. cherchèrent à s'agripper

as he let in the clutch[1]. The smart red sports car gave a growl and swept off[2].

Alice became aware[3] of the press watching curiously from outside the courtyard and some of the hotel servants watching as well.

She picked up her case and, with her head held high[4], she walked back into the hotel.

Hamish and Charlie rowed slowly back to Lochdubh after an afternoon's fishing. They had caught four mackerel and two ling[5]. Charlie had lost his hard, calculating stare and was looking out at the world with dreamy pleasure.

'There's Mr Johnson waiting for you,' he said as they approached the shore.

Hamish was sharply reminded of the time when they had last returned and Blair was waiting for them.

'Where have you been?' asked Mr Johnson as soon as Hamish landed on the beach. 'I've been going out of my wits[6]. That girl Alice Wilson had a scene with Mr Blythe and she's disappeared. Her case is still at the reception and she hasn't booked in for[7] another night. The staff have been out searching for her.'

'You run along home,' said Hamish to the boy. 'Don't worry, Mr Johnson. I'll find her.'

'Where would she go?' thought Hamish as he drove up the twisting road out of Lochdubh. 'I suppose she might just keep on walking and walking.'

He drove on through the pale Highland twilight, his eyes searching from left to right of the road.

He was ten miles out of Lochdubh when his sharp[8] eyes suddenly spied[9] what looked like a

1. embrayait
2. fila
3. prit conscience
4. la tête haute
5. juliennes
6. ne sais plus à quel saint me vouer
7. réservé
8. perçants
9. aperçurent

black lump[1] on a black rock. He drove on and parked the car around a bend in the road. Then he began to walk back to the rock, his shoes making no noise on the springy heather[2]. Alice sat on the rock, a picture[3] of abject misery[4]. She was not crying, having cried all day until she could cry no more, but she was hiccupping with dry sobs[5].

Hamish sat down beside her. 'Only a fool would cry for someone who didn't really want them.'

'Go away,' said Alice, turning red-rimmed[6] eyes to his.

'No, I will not go away. You are coming with me. You have caused enough worry and trouble this day. And all over some pipsqueak[7] you didn't even love.'

'I love him,' wailed[8] Alice.

'No, you don't. Went to bed with him, didn't you? Aye, I thought as much[9]. So now you've got to pretend you love him. Och, lassie[10], it's your pride[11] that's hurt, not your heart. There's one silly woman charged with murder and all because of damned snobbery and here you are planning to jump in the nearest loch as soon as you get up the courage so as to make a rat like Blythe sorry[12].'

'I ... I didn't ... I wouldn't.'

'Look, I tried to tell you he was a snob. As soon as he decided Daphne was rich enough, he decided to settle for her[13]. She'll marry him. That kind always get what they want and they'll have a dead-alive[14] sort of marriage. You only wanted the dream, Alice. Be honest and admit it's over[15].'

'What if I'm pregnant?'

'Face that when it comes[16]. When's your next period[17]?' asked Hamish.

'Next week, I think.'

1. masse
2. bruyère moelleuse
3. incarnation
4. indicible douleur
5. hoquetait sans larmes
6. ourlés de rouge
7. freluquet
8. geignit
9. c'est ce que je pensais
10. Ah ma fille
11. orgueil
12. pour donner des remords à cette ordure de Blythe
13. s'est décidé en sa faveur à elle
14. très morne
15. que c'est fini
16. Vous verrez bien à ce moment-là
17. vos prochaines règles

'Well, you'll maybe just be all right. Come along with me and I'll get us a drink. You're a pretty girl and you're young.'

'Do ... do you think I'm pretty?'

'Very,' lied[1] Hamish gallantly. 'Smashing little thing[2], that's what I thought when I first saw you.'

He helped her to her feet[3] and put an arm about her shoulders and together they walked towards the road.

'It's a grand evening to be alive,' said Hamish. 'Just think about that.'

Down below them, the lights of the village twinkled[4] in the half dark. The twilight was scented with thyme and pine and heather. A rocketing pheasant whirred up[5] from a clump[6] of heather at the other side of the road. Out in the loch, the fishing boats were chugging out to sea[7].

Hamish pulled Alice to the side of the road as he heard a car approaching. A Rolls, black and sleek[8], slowed. Inside sat Priscilla Halburton-Smythe. She was wearing a white evening dress and a diamond necklace sparkled against her breast. Beside her at the wheel[9] was John Harrington. Priscilla looked at Hamish, at Hamish's arm about Alice's shoulders, shrugged[10], and said something to John, who looked across her at Hamish and Alice and laughed. Then the car sped away.

Alice took a deep breath of clean-scented air. She was feeling better already. Hamish's arm was comforting. She glanced up at him. He really wasn't bad-looking[11]. His eyelashes were very long for a man and his hair was a fascinating colour of red. 'You're right,' said Alice. 'Only a fool would cry for someone who didn't really want them.'

1. mentit
2. Jolie petite nana
3. à se relever
4. clignotait
5. faisan s'éleva en flèche dans un bruit d'ailes
6. massif
7. sortaient en mer en pétaradant
8. élégante
9. au volant
10. haussa les épaules
11. laid

Hamish watched the tail lights[1] of the disappearing Rolls-Royce. 'Did I say that?' he asked, and then added in so low a voice[2] that Alice could not hear what he was saying, 'If I said that then I am a very great fool indeed.'

He helped Alice into his car but he sat for a few moments, staring straight ahead.

'I've always wondered, Mr Macbeth,' said Alice timidly. 'What's a FEB?'

Hamish let in the clutch. 'Fucking English Bastard[3],' he said. And with an angry screech of tyres[4] he swung the car around and they plunged down into the heathery darkness of the road leading to Lochdubh.

1. feux arrière
2. à voix si basse
3. un putain d'Anglais
4. dans un violent crissement de pneus,

La collection Yes you can!

Les faux débutants

Linwood Barclay	*Broken Promise*
M. C. Beaton	*Agatha Raisin and the Quiche of Death* ✦ *Agatha Raisin and the Vicious Vet* ✦ *Agatha Raisin and the Potted Gardener* ✦ *Death of a Gossip*
Harlan Coben	*The Stranger*
Michael Connelly	*The Black Box* ✦ *The Burning Room* ✦ *The Drop* ✦ *The Wrong Side of Goodbye*
Ken Follett	*The Modigliani Scandal*
Mary Higgins Clark	*A Cry in the Night* *A Stranger is Watching* *Loves Music, Loves to Dance* *Where are the Children?*
Anthony Horowitz	*The House of Silk*
George R. R. Martin	*The Hedge Knight* ✦ *The Sworn Sword* ✦ *The Mystery Knight*
Ian Rankin	*In a House of Lies* ✦ *Knots & Crosses*
Nicholas Sparks	*Message in a Bottle*

Les intermédiaires

Harlan Coben	*Caught* ✦ *Play Dead* ✦ *Stay Close* ✦ *Tell No One* ✦ *The Woods*
Ken Follett	*Paper Money*
Anthony Horowitz	*Moriarty*
P. D. James	*A Mind to Murder* ✦ *Death Comes to Pemberley*
Douglas Kennedy	*The Big Picture*
Stephen King	*Finders Keepers* ✦ *The Green Mile*
John le Carré	*A Most Wanted Man*

Les avancés

Paul Auster	*Leviathan* ✦ *Oracle Night* ✦
Julian Barnes	*The Sense of an Ending*
Michael Cunningham	*By Nightfall* ✦ *The Hours*
Helen Fielding	*Bridget Jones's Diary* ✦ *Bridget Jones: The Edge of Reason*
Elizabeth George	*A Great Deliverance*
Stephen King	*Dolores Claiborne* ✦ *Misery*

Les classiques

Jane Austen	*Northanger Abbey* ✦ *Pride and Prejudice*
Charlotte Brontë	*Jane Eyre*
G. K. Chesterton	*The Innocence of Father Brown*
Arthur Conan Doyle	*A Study in Scarlet* ✦ *Five Adventures of Sherlock Holmes* ✦ *The Hound of the Baskervilles*
Francis Scott Fitzgerald	*Tender is the Night* ✦ *The Great Gatsby*
Washington Irving, A. Conan Doyle, Edgar Allan Poe	*The Legend of Sleepy Hollow* *and Other Scary Stories*
H. P. Lovecraft	*The Call of Cthulhu and Other Weird Stories*
George Orwell	*Animal Farm* ✦ *1984*
Edgar Allan Poe	*The Fall of the House of Usher* *and Other Scary Stories*
Mary Shelley	*Frankenstein*
Bram Stoker	*Dracula*
Edith Wharton	*The Age of Innocence*
Oscar Wilde	*The Importance of Being Earnest* ✦ *The Picture of Dorian Gray*
Virginia Woolf	*To the Lighthouse*

HARRAP'S
YES YOU CAN!
OSCAR WILDE
The Importance of Being Earnest
Idéal pour réussir le BAC
Texte intégral en VO
Pour lire en anglais avec la traduction des mots-clés